Wood's Harbor

Steven Becker

The White Marlin Press
whitemarlinpress.com

Wood's Harbor

ONE

Mac swatted the no-see-ums swarming around his face and rubbed his salt-crusted eyes. The coating felt like sandpaper. Finally he removed enough of the crystals to squeeze one eye open. The glare of the sun made him close it immediately. He tried to move, but his legs resisted the effort. It took him a long minute to realize they were entwined in mangrove branches and covered with debris. It was a struggle to sit up, so he lifted his knees instead, and in the process gained enough wiggle room to slide out of his cocoon. He forced himself to squint through his one good eye and crawled across the muck to the tide line where he splashed water on his face. It was salt water, but it was wet. He continued until he was able to open both eyes.

His vision was clouded from the salt and sun, but he forced himself to survey his situation. Surrounded by mangrove roots, he saw pieces of the wreckage in the brush and tried to remember what had happened. He gazed up at the sun, high in the sky, and realized it had been close to sunset the day before when time had stopped; he had been out for almost eighteen hours. His memory came back in bits and pieces as he moved above the high tide line and sat amidst the tangle of roots and brush to think about the last few days. It came back slowly. He remembered the sailboat fighting each wave as he tried to steer it into the raging Gulf Stream. Then the rest of the memory flooded back, startling him to alertness.

He gained his feet and looked around for Mel and Armando. They had been with him on the boat, but his last memory was the life raft and

1

the terrified looks on their faces. The mast had snapped, taking his attention away from the drifting lifeboat. That was all he could remember. The trio had escaped the corrupt CIA agent and headed to the Bahamas, a trail of dead bodies and destruction behind them, a 'borrowed' sailboat beneath them. It had been his insistence on running that had left him stranded and his stubbornness that had convinced him he could navigate the huge waves and current of the Gulf Stream. He looked around with remorse. It may have cost Mel and Armando their lives.

Mac pushed the thought from his mind and tried to gain his feet. His arms and legs were covered with open cuts and scrapes, the current target of the invisible bugs, but his wounds showed no sign of infection. He was forced to crawl, the dense vegetation not allowing him to rise. With two choices, the open water or the brush, he chose the water. There was likely a search going on and he would have to be careful to remain out of sight. If he was found on US soil, he would surely be arrested.

First on the list would be the poaching charge. He recalled the image of the heiress, Cayenne Cannady, red hair ablaze, as she burned at the smuggler's haven. The temptress had suckered his friend and first mate, Trufante, into using his boat to poach lobsters. The black cloud that followed the Cajun mate was above them that day. The pair had been caught, the boat traced to Mac and confiscated along with his house. He shook his head. Focus on the present. It was better to stay invisible until he could figure things out. He worked through the brush to the shore but couldn't get the two faces in the lifeboat out of his mind. The question of whether he was responsible for Mel's death dominated his thoughts.

The winds had calmed, reducing the seas to a light chop. From the debris scattered in the mangroves, he could tell it had been a good blow. Parts of a boat, fishing nets, plastic bottles and trash were scattered in a wavy line along the tide mark or in the branches, some, two feet off the ground, where the surge from the wind-blown waves had deposited them. He looked around for anything useful and found a pair of mismatched flip-flops and a half-full water bottle which he drained. Able to stand now, he set his shoulders and lower back into a stretch. The sun had moved behind him. He knew he was somewhere back in the Keys facing the Atlantic Ocean. There were hundreds of miles of mangrove-covered shores in the island chain running from Homestead through Key Largo, past Key West to the Dry Tortugas, and he had no idea just where he had been marooned.

He turned towards the sun and started half-walking and half-wading west through the mud, the best choice as he figured the six-knot current of the Gulf Stream would have pushed the wreckage north or east. At least he was still in the Keys. The last place he needed to enter civilization was Miami or points north. He had been walking for an hour, by the position of the sun, but doubted he had covered more than a mile. He fought for each inch. Finally he saw a high-rise appear over the brush and sighed in relief as he recognized the lone condo standing guard over the entrance to Key Colony Beach. He studied the shoreline and moved back into the cover of the brush as a boat appeared from the inlet, then looked inland to find a place to rest until sunset. Coco Plumb Beach, the long stretch of sand leading to the channel, was too busy to approach in the daylight. Even if he wasn't identified, he looked like a hobo and would be reported by the residents.

He crawled under the cover of a small tree. His thoughts turned inward as he fought hunger and thirst. The initial shock had worn off. He could feel every scrape on his body, salt stinging open wounds as it dried. Mel was back in his thoughts. Had she survived? Where was she? Armando was a concern, but he would be handled as a political refugee, given the best care American taxpayers could afford. Mel would be treated as a criminal. He waited for the sun to set, knowing there was only one place he could go for help - and that always led to trouble.

TWO

The light of the near-full moon woke Mac from a sound sleep. He was disoriented. As a fisherman, he knew where the moon was at all times, its phase and movement synchronized in his mind. In his current state he was having a hard enough time figuring out where he was - never mind the moon. He sat up and tried to remember the last time he was certain of the orb's travels; the day before, he thought, when he had left Wood's Island with Mel and Armando.

The memory of the island in flames, an act of retribution from the CIA man and the smuggler was not one he cared to dwell on. After a few minutes he pieced together it was near midnight. Time meant nothing to him with darkness to conceal his movements. He still had to be careful; the moon was bright enough to cast shadows. It was the tide he was more concerned with. Navigating the murky waters would be best accomplished during slack tide. At low tide, too much shoreline would be revealed, forcing him into the open to avoid the muddy pitfalls along the shoreline. High tide would bring water to the brush line, forcing him to swim.

He took his time, carefully stretching to check for damage as he rose. His muscles and joints were stiff, and stung from the cuts on his arms and legs, but all his parts worked. With no fresh water he forced saliva into his mouth to satisfy his thirst and started off towards the lights from the high-rise, using the building as a landmark. He was on Deer Key, best he could tell, and he looked at the small, mangrove-covered island to the West, the glow of Marathon visible behind it. He moved along the tide line, head down to avoid the mucky potholes that could suck him in like quicksand. Mullet jumped, breaking the silence, the fish traveling in small pods; no concern to anyone except the tarpon that chased them onto the flats. He flinched when a leathery fin brushed him and started to slide his feet, rather than lift them, to avoid the barbs of the stingrays foraging in the shallow water.

Step by step, he moved towards open water to reach the smaller Key, holding the flip-flops in his hand, setting each foot carefully in case of a coral head or unexpected hole, the ink-black waters hiding hazards clearly visible in daylight. Fortunately the water never reached higher than his knees as he crossed the flats between the islands. The backside of the Key was desolate except for the white ibises roosted in the mangroves. He reached shore and made his way around the island to avoid the dredged canal leading to several houses and docks.

The lights from the houses on the nearby Key to the west looked inviting, but he knew he had to take the harder route and steeled himself as he entered the mangrove-lined channel that led to the mainland. It would be a long, hard mile, but he wanted to reach the anonymity of US 1. Coco Plumb Drive on the adjacent Key was the easier route, just a few hundred feet away, but it was too quiet, and probably patrolled by security cars. If he could reach the busier, more commercial highway connecting Miami and the mainland to Key West, he could hide in plain sight, looking like every other hobo in paradise.

The walk soon turned into mindless monotony after the lights became obscured by mangroves. He trudged along, caution fading; the water too shallow for anything except a flats boat, and there was no reason for any to be here at night. Daylight found the flats often crowded with the shallow draft boats searching for bonefish; the prize, referred to as ghosts during the day, were totally invisible at night. Most night-time fishing activity centered around the bridges. Any boat or man found here at night would be up to no good.

Thoughts of Mel came flooding back and the list of all the things he had done wrong in the last week ran like movie credits in front of his eyes. Surely he could have left her out of it, but her own stubborn streak would not allow her to sit on the sidelines, especially after she found Cayenne Cannady, the trust fund heiress she had been doing pro bono work for, was involved. Cannady had seemed honest at first, but her coral farm and flamboyant lifestyle were sucking her trust fund dry. Desperate to maintain her standing, she was forced to forge an alliance with a smuggler to harvest illegal lobsters from the coral farm. Once Mel found the connection, she wouldn't back down an inch until justice was served. Regardless of how she got involved, he still felt responsible for her as well as Armando, the Cuban baseball player. His head was still fuzzy as he tried to put together all the pieces, but he remembered he and Mel had rescued Armando from the smugglers.

He guessed he had been wading almost an hour when he saw the first headlights through the brush. An empty plastic water bottle floated by. Instead of being angry for the defilement of his paradise, it did nothing but remind him of his thirst. He picked up his pace. The ground became firmer with each step as he crawled out of the brush at eye level with the asphalt, the built-up heat of the day shimmering from its surface. Limestone road base crunched under the worn flip-flops now back on his feet. He climbed the embankment in a crouch, ducking as several trucks towing boats blew past him and he waited until an opening appeared. He hobbled across the road, reaching the other side and the seclusion of the frontage road before the next set of headlights approached, then crossed to the far side of the narrow road running parallel to the highway. More exposed than he would have liked, he started in the direction of Marathon, but found himself getting weaker with each step. It was probably two in the morning, but that didn't stop the August humidity, vicious even at night, from sapping whatever little reserves he had left.

One step at a time was all he could think about. He marched into the dark night: one foot, then the other. He knew he needed water and a place to rest, but with no boat or home, the only refuge he could trust was his wayward mate, Trufante, and he was several miles away. Finally he reached a point where he could no longer continue and was about to sit down on the street and give in to whatever was about to take hold of him when he saw the first sign of life ahead.

The sign was weatherworn and barely legible, but he knew what it was. After twenty years of traveling the only artery connecting the island chain, it didn't take long to memorize every business. The yard was set well back from the road, but he had been here several times looking for boat parts. Mac waited for traffic before he crossed the frontage road and the highway. He climbed over the gate, entered the yard of the dry dock facility and walked between two rows of boats; inspecting each one for a place he could take refuge. He stopped at a sport-fisher set on blocks, an aluminum ladder standing by its transom.

It was not unusual for live-aboards to continue to stay on their boats when they were in dry dock, but from what he remembered, this boatyard didn't offer the showers and bathroom facilities they needed when their boats were being serviced. There should be no one here, and with a quick glance in each direction, he started up the ladder and climbed over the transom. The deck was torn up, revealing a large fuel tank that he carefully skirted as he made his way to the cabin. He grasped the doorknob and slowly turned the handle. The door opened. He entered the cockpit, finding a control station on the right and a small galley on the left. His thirst drove him to the sink, where hoping the batteries were still good, he turned on the faucet. Water dribbled from the spout and he put his head under the small stream.

He drank his fill and washed his face before searching the cabinets for food. The refrigerator was warm and empty, but he found some crackers and peanut butter in a cabinet. After clearing the table, he sat and started to eat. Just as he was getting comfortable, something brushed against his leg. He jumped but recognized the furry outline of a cat and continued to eat. The cat coiled and landed onto the bench besides him. It started to meow and Mac succumbed, alternating crackers with it. The food exhausted, he went back to the faucet and drank before lying down on the bunk. He wasn't sure of his next move, but without some rest, there wouldn't be one. The cat settled into a ball by his head, and with no energy to shoo it away, he left it.

***

Voices startled him awake, what he thought was just a few minutes later, but when he raised his head to look where the sound was coming from, he saw daylight streaming through the curtains.

"Well, they found the girl and some Cuban refugee floating in a life raft. I think they're about to call off the search for that low-life Travis character. Don't guess he's worth looking for."

"He ain't all bad. Just has a habit of getting mixed up in the wrong kind of things. They're saying the woman's in intensive care. Wonder what they do with Cubans these days?"

Mac's heart beat hard in his chest at the news of Mel.

"Political sanctuary, probably; he's probably out at the Krome

Processing Center up in Miami getting groomed to be an American."

Mac had heard all he needed to. He slid away from the door towards the V berth in the bow of the boat. The last thing he needed was to be discovered. He stood, released the latch on the hatch above the berth, and slowly pushed it open. The cabin would provide enough cover to crawl out the small opening and onto the deck, but getting off the boat was not going to be so easy. The cat moved around his ankles. He was about to kick it away when he got an idea and lifted it through the hatch. The men were still bickering about bad gas, the boat owner threatening lawsuits for collusion and fraud, when Mac pulled himself through the opening and crept forward on the deck. He looked over the railing; the ground was at least eight feet below, too far to jump without being noticed. With a whispered apology, he picked up the cat and hurled it towards the stern, hoping that cats did indeed always land on their feet. It squealed on impact and he grabbed the rail and hoisted himself over the bow, dropping to the ground with a thud.

The men were still going back and forth, apparently making some kind of a deal. He crawled on all fours into the brush, crouched, and waited while they finished their negotiation. The men moved towards the office and although they were out of sight there was nowhere for him to go. The daylight was his enemy and he eyed the other boats lining the road, finally selecting a sailboat clearly in need of maintenance. He went towards it, finding the cat at his heels, and couldn't help but smile. Without a thought, he lifted it onto the deck of the boat before climbing the swim ladder behind it.

THREE

Mac lay on the bunk sweating in the hot cabin, his mind churning through the possibilities. The vents did little to disperse the heat. He had tried the small fan by his head, but the boat's batteries were long dead. Sleep eluded him and he tossed and turned for what seemed like hours, before finally giving up and searching the boat for anything that might prove useful. For what, he didn't know. Somehow he needed to see Mel and get his life back on track, but beyond finding Trufante, he had no next step.

He prowled through the cabinets and holds, making a small pile on the table of anything more useful than the lint in his pockets. The boat was in rough shape and he didn't think the owner would miss anything. Houses age, but boats decay, every day a little more, until they reach the point of no return, where it takes a complete overhaul to refurbish them. This boat fit that bill. It looked abandoned; the once proud owner had probably stopped paying the storage payments some time ago and the boat would continue to rot until the yard needed the space.

Under the bench seat he found an open case of water. It looked old, but even if it had an expiration date, he would have ignored it. He took a bottle, drained it, then opened another and resumed his search. A cabinet yielded some cans of tuna and beans. He set them on the table and prowled through the drawers, where he found an opener, and sat with the curtains drawn, eating, thinking and sweating. After finishing, he examined what he had collected from his search: matches, a small knife, and a few dollars in loose change. He slid the curtains enough to gauge the height of the sun in the sky and guessed it was about noon. With no choice but to wait, he found an old John D. MacDonald novel and spent the afternoon with Travis MacGee.

***

The cabin was in the shadow of the adjacent boat when he opened his eyes and realized he must have fallen asleep. He made his way to the head and used the contents of one of the water bottles to wash. A quick search of the cabinets in the berth upgraded his wardrobe to a clean T-shirt and shorts. An old Marlins ball cap caught his attention. Though not a hat fan, he decided to take it. By the time he washed and dressed, the sun had reached the horizon. He prepared to move out.

With two water bottles stuffed in the outer pockets of his cargo shorts, he loaded the small cache of supplies in the other pockets. He crept up the companionway and stuck his head out to look for any activity. The yard was quiet and he went to the transom, climbed down the swim ladder, and after scanning the yard, walked towards the road. The cat reappeared, meowing for attention, but he ignored it, pulled down the bill of the hat over his face, and stepped onto US 1. Twilight was rush hour in the Keys, with trucks pulling boats both ways and half-baked drunk tourists cruising bars and gift shops.

The traffic was heavy and he waited for an opening before crossing the highway. Back on the frontage road, he started walking west towards Marathon. Fisherman's Hospital, where he suspected Mel was, and Trufante's apartment both lay in that direction. He kept an eye on the road while he walked, twice ducking into the bushes when he saw Highway Patrol cars. An old International Travelall passed by and he wished he were close enough to flag down the driver. Jesse McDermitt owned the beast and lived on his own island, close to Wood's place out by the Content Keys. Jesse was an acquaintance but, unlike a lot of the Keys' residents, was dependable. He could have helped and Mac racked his brain for some way to contact the reclusive ex-Marine. He could often be found at the Rusty Anchor, but Mac didn't want to risk being seen. Rusty, the owner, could be trusted though, and Mac thought about sneaking around back after closing for a quick conversation.

He decided on using Rusty as a backup plan, sticking with Trufante as his first option. The Cajun was already intertwined in the poaching scam and was ultimately responsible for the whole mess by getting conned into using his boat. He was trouble but Mac knew him inside and out. The man wouldn't judge him and if he could help, he would. The frontage road turned into the Heritage Trail, a walking and biking path, as he reached the airport, but it wasn't much more than a sidewalk. He was less worried about being recognized now. Most of the characters he knew would be in bars, not out walking or biking. He only had to cross one intersection before he turned right on the first street and walked towards the small apartment building, hoping the Cajun was home.

Mac heard the party before he saw it and knew trouble was brewing. He reached the two-story apartment building and stopped behind a clump of sago palms planted near a cluster of mailboxes. People were on the balconies, in the pool, and overflowing into the parking lot. As he had suspected, the center of activity was none other than Trufante's apartment. He crouched down and finished the last of his water and watched the action, but the tall Cajun, easily recognizable with his lanky frame and grin resembling a Cadillac's grille, was nowhere to be seen. Mac waited, wondering how to find him without being recognized. He also had to wonder why Trufante was having a party when Mel was in the hospital and he was supposed to be lost at sea. Another piece of his memory returned and he recalled giving him the dual engine go-fast boat to use as a decoy. Somehow he was sure that was tied to the party.

***

Norm leaned back into the plush couch as the girl swayed above him. He thought the strip club would take his mind off his problems, but the harsh music and lights were only increasing his headache. The song finished and the girl stepped off the couch and accepted the twenty-dollar bill, giving him a contemptuous glance as if it should have been more. Without a second look, she moved on to the next group of men, hoping for better prey. Norm leaned forward, drained his drink, got up and walked to the door.

Duval Street, the partying heart of Key West, was just picking up steam. He stood in the entry to the club watching the scene. Tourists and locals of all flavors were milling about, many drinking openly from red Solo cups. Usually he enjoyed nights like this, but in his current mood, he knew he was not destined to have fun. He asked the bouncer to hail a taxi, and when the pink cab pulled to the curb, the large tattooed man opened the back door, not willing to close it until Norm had laid a five in his palm. He gave the driver the name of his hotel, sat back and tried to ignore the party on the street flashing by the tinted windows. At the hotel, he paid the driver and got out on his own, refusing to be the victim of another door-opener. Relief came over him as he entered the air-conditioned lobby and found the elevator.

He stayed to the side of the hallway away from the cameras, burying his head in his shoulder in the event they caught his face. It never hurt to be careful, he thought, and after a glance in each direction, he unlocked the door, quickly closing it behind him. Crossing the room, he stood in front of the floor-to-ceiling window and stared out.

His room overlooked the Atlantic Ocean and he stared at the small waves lit by the moon, a sight most tourists paid extra for. Like everything else, tonight it did nothing for him. He closed the curtains, sat at the desk and opened the military-grade laptop. The computer started up and he entered his password. When his desktop appeared, he clicked the CIA portal and entered another password to access the main screen. He held his breath, hoping the world had remained intact since he had last checked, clicked the email tab and waited while the messages downloaded. There were several hundred, about average for two days, and he started to sort through them. Anything he was Cc'd on, he left for later, and started opening the emails that were addressed to only him. Anything with another name on it, unless it was the President, would be handled by someone else. Two messages stood out.

One had a satellite image of a fire on a small island. He smacked the desktop when he realized it was his accomplice Jay's hideout. The refuge of the smuggler, hidden in the back country of the Keys, had been torched, and someone was taunting him with it. A glance at the sender confirmed the email was clearly from a fake address and rerouted through several internet providers. He knew he could task Alicia with finding out who sent the message. The over-eager analyst was constantly hinting that she wanted field work and would do anything to get out of the office, but her idea of 'anything' and his were most likely different. A shame, he thought, fantasizing for a moment about her. But that would take time, and though her skills were impressive, it would involve resources that didn't need to know about the island and fire. In his two years behind a desk, he had made more enemies than friends in the halls of Langley and many would delight in ruining his career. His friends and allies were still in the field, where he wished he still worked.

He deleted the message and looked again at the sender and subject line of the other email. It was sent through a Guerrilla Mail account, a private email server that erased messages upon delivery. Unlike the trash bin on a computer, for a small fee these messages were permanently gone. He opened the message, still unsure of the sender, but intrigued by the subject line: Key West to Havana Ferry. The message had no text, only 0600, which he guessed was a time, and two sets of numbers which he knew were GPS coordinates. After studying the numbers, he realized they were nearby. An uneasy feeling came over him. Whoever sent the message knew he was in Key West, something he had not told his office. He liked to be on the side, dishing out the intrigue - not taking it.

He wrote the coordinates on a hotel note pad, closed the email program and opened an incognito browser window where he entered the numbers and waited as the globe focused on the northern tip of a small Key to the west. Most people thought the Keys ended at the painted buoy marking the southernmost point of the continental US, but in fact the island chain extended another seventy miles to the Dry Tortugas. He had to assume whoever sent the satellite picture of the island also sent this email, and he had no choice but to go. In all likelihood, this was a one way email that would bounce any response. He could either show up or not, but the lure was too much to refuse.

In another window he googled the Key West to Havana ferry and scanned the first page in the results. The first trip, a landmark in the new atmosphere of cooperation between the US and Cuba, was due to depart in two days. The Obama administration had lifted travel restrictions to the island and the ferry was the first of several scheduled to run between Havana and Tampa, Ft. Lauderdale and Miami. But unlike many Cuban-Americans, he didn't want the restrictions to be lifted just yet. He had other plans.

Right now, he needed to forget the last few days. He went to the mini-bar, took out two bottles of Scotch, poured them into a water glass, drained half and took the remainder to the desk. He closed the web browser and returned to the CIA portal where he navigated to the section on Cuba and the Caribbean. The window opened and he sipped his drink, scanning the latest reports and articles. He quickly bored of the research, finished his drink and set the alarm on his phone to three am, cursing whoever he was going to meet for the early hour, wondering what the urgency and secrecy was all about. He tossed and turned, then gave up sleep, checked his email one more time, packed his possessions and left the room.

It might have been morning to him, but the party still raged in Key West and tourists were streaming in and out of the lobby, keeping the night alive. It was easy to blend into the scenery until he reached the front door, where he grabbed the first cab he saw and gave directions to the marina.

FOUR

Mac saw the streak of blue in Annie's hair from behind the cluster of palms and watched her mingle, waiting for an opening to get her alone. The barmaid sipped from a can of Coke instead of the beer bottles or red Solo cups the rest of the crowd had. He guessed she must be going to work. With the bill of the cap pulled down to hide his face, he made his move when she left the group she was talking to. Catching up to her on the way to the street, he looped his arm in hers and walked her back to his hiding spot by the mailboxes.

"I thought that was you," she said. "Half the county's out looking for your body and I got to tell you a lot of them don't care if it's dead or alive."

"Nice to see you too," Mac said, then decided there was no reason to antagonize her if he needed her cooperation. He changed his tone of voice. "Where's Trufante and what's with the party?"

"Heck if I know. Tru comes into the bar last night flashing a pile of hundreds. Buying drinks and talking large about this killer party he's throwing."

"Didn't happen to say where he got the money?" Mac asked, although he already suspected the source.

"You know that no one asks questions around here."

Mac nodded, knowing the unwritten code of the Keys. The island chain had retained its heritage of pirates and smugglers. When the fish weren't biting or the economy was down, taking the tourists with it, the residents had to do what they had to do. "Where's he at?"

"Made a run down to Key West for supplies." She giggled.

"Crap. I need to find him," Mac said, worried about damage control, rather than information. Someone would surely take notice of Trufante throwing money around and further increase the mess he was in. "Where'd he go?"

She shrugged. "I'd guess somewhere on Duval."

Mac thought for a minute. "I know where he probably is. How long ago did he leave?"

"About half an hour," she said.

He had just missed him. "Any chance you can help me out? I need to find him now. If you're going to work, can I drop you and use your car?"

She looked at him, "Never could say no to either of you." She was quiet for a minute. "Aren't you going to ask about Mel?"

"I heard she was in intensive care. Not much I can do there. The minute I walk through the door of the hospital, they'll lock me up and throw away the key." He looked at the ground. "Wish there was more I could do to help."

She left the concealment of the small palm trees and started walking away. "You coming?"

Mac looked around and went after her. They walked out to the road where cars were parked haphazardly on the grass shoulder in an attempt to avoid the puddles of rain water. He followed her to a ten-year-old yellow Jeep. She tossed him the keys. He got in the driver's seat, adjusted it to fit his six-foot frame, and waited for her to climb in the passenger side. A more discreet car would have been better, but he wasn't in a position to negotiate. He started the engine, pulled onto US 1, and drove the mile to the bar.

"Really appreciate this," he called after her.

She turned, "Just bring it back in one piece. I get off around two."

Mac waited until she was inside, and then started out of the lot. There was a moment's hesitation when he thought about turning left, the direction of the hospital, but they would be looking for him. It hurt, but he knew he had to find Trufante, shut down the party, and figure things out. The Seven Mile Bridge appeared, its long spans disappearing into the water, and a strange feeling passed over him, relieved he was out of Marathon where he was well known. Although they were spread out over a hundred and twenty miles, the Keys were a small, tight-knit community. He and Wood had built many of the bridges connecting the islands and were known throughout the chain, but Marathon had been his home base.

It was OK to let them think he was dead. It might even be better. No one would suspect he was working to clear his name. His house had been destroyed by a rocket-propelled grenade, his boat confiscated, and Wood's Island was on fire the last he saw it. Dead was probably better than alive for him right now. The pieces of the puzzle were moving around in his head and he almost forgot to slow down when he entered Big Pine Key, home of the Key deer refuge and biggest speed trap in the Keys. He drove through Little Torch, Ramrod, and Summerland Keys, watching his rear-view mirror the entire time. Once he reached Cudjoe Key, he relaxed and started to think again.

The CIA man was the missing link. He was the only one that had enough to lose, and enough juice to get his name cleared. He just needed to find the right lever to pull to get his attention. The man, he suspected, was not directly involved with Cannady and the smuggler, Jay, at least in the poaching scam. His particular sideline was smuggling baseball players from Cuba. So in the twisted world of deceit, there was no reason for them to be enemies.

He reached Stock Island and thought of Armando - that he might be the key. The Cuban player was the only one that could implicate the CIA man directly. If Mac could reach him first, he would have something to negotiate with. The detention center, where the men in the boatyard had said he was being held, was just south of Miami. He thought about turning around, but knocking on the door of a federal facility at midnight was not staying under the radar. Tomorrow would do. For now, he decided to keep the plan the plan and find Trufante.

He crossed the Stock Island Bridge and entered Key West, turned right and followed North Roosevelt past several new chain stores and the Garrison Bight Harbor. At White Street, he turned right again and entered an old residential neighborhood, the streets lined with the colorful Victorian homes the island was known for. He reached Eaton Street and turned left. The activity level picked up the closer he came to Duval and a few blocks short of the famous drag, he considered himself lucky when he found a parking spot.

Head down and cap pulled over his face, although he didn't think he'd be recognized here, he walked to the entrance of the Turtle. The watering hole, a few blocks off the main street, was more subdued than the louder haunts over on Duval and favored locals over tourists. He entered and looked down the standing room only bar. Trufante stood out like a sore thumb; not only the tallest, he was also the loudest, and if neither of those features attracted your attention his teeth resembled the grille of a mid-sixties Cadillac when he opened his mouth and showed his thousand-dollar smile. Mac looked at him and gathered from the drawn look and rings under his eyes that this wasn't the first night of the bender. Sideways, he squeezed through the crowd and stood in front of the Cajun.

"Mac freakin' Travis," Trufante greeted him, one hand on his beer bottle.

Mac was out of patience. He reached for Trufante's empty hand appearing to shake it, but grabbed it, forced the elbow to bend and swung the arm behind Trufante's back. The big man winced and Mac backed off slightly, but kept enough pressure to walk him out of the bar.

"Easy, buddy," Trufante said once they reached the sidewalk. "There's half a hundred sitting on the bar in there."

Mac kept his grip and pushed the man into the alley adjacent to the bar. Near the back door and sheltered by the dumpster, he released his grip. "You need to tell me what's going on right now."

"Well, hell. You're alive."

"Was that party back at your house your twisted idea of a wake?" Mac growled. Trufante's easy going manner could try his patience at the best of times, and these were far from that. "Where's the money from?"

"Shit! That what's up? Never mind then. You gave me Commando's boat to lead the diversion, right. Told me to do with it what I could. Well, the last thing I need is for one of his buddies to see me running that boat, so I took off down here and sold it to a dude I know that chops them up."

Mac relaxed slightly. Although he was throwing around the proceeds of the sale like a drunken sailor, he had to admit that selling the boat was a good idea. In the islands, where there were as many boats as cars, boat theft was not uncommon. The problem was that many boats were easy to identify. Commando's was an eye-catcher with its three monster outboards mounted on the tail end of the cigarette-style hull. Similar to the shops that cut up cars for parts, underground businesses did the same for boats here. Swap the engines, repaint the hull, and change some of the noticeable features, like T-tops and rocket launchers, and you had a new boat.

"Maybe you did the right thing. But you can't be throwing the money around."

He nodded, but Mac was sure the reasoning was lost on the free spirit.

"What about Mel? Have you seen her?"

Trufante shook his head. "Went by there, but they got a new sheriff in town. Mean old boy come down from somewhere up North to take over for Jules. Big ol' sucker was sitting right in front of her room. I took one look and high-tailed it out of there."

"What happened to Jules?" Mac asked.

"Guess you haven't seen a paper or heard the news. She resigned. Between the fires and the bodies, it was more than she could explain."

Mac stared at the ground, thinking about the collateral damage to his friend. She had gone out of her way to help him and now was out of a job. "Where's she at?"

He shrugged his shoulders. "The last thing I do is keep an eye on the law if the law isn't keeping an eye on me. Probably holed up with that girlfriend of hers. Heard she got work in Miami."

Mac remembered Heather. Maybe he should track her down and apologize to Jules. Or maybe it was better just to stay dead. "We gotta go," Mac started walking to where he had parked.

"What about my bike?"

"Stash it. You're in no condition to drive anyway. The last thing I need is for you to start singing the blues in jail." Mac continued to walk, looking over his shoulder every few steps to make sure Trufante was behind him. They reached Annie's Jeep and climbed in. "First thing is to shut down that party of yours before that new sheriff realizes it's you and makes your acquaintance. I heard those North Florida crackers are some tough bastards." It was hard for outsiders to understand, but the further north you went in Florida, the further south you got. Most towns north of Orlando, especially in the interior, were right out of *Deliverance*.

"What then?" Trufante asked as he tried to fit his frame into the passenger seat.

"Where's the boat at?"

Trufante squinted at him.

"You did the right thing getting rid of it, but there was a bag I stashed on it that might come in handy about now," Mac said. He looked at his empty wrist. "What time is it?"

Trufante took his phone from the pocket of his cargo pants and glanced at the screen. "It's almost eleven. Figure this time of day it takes an hour and a half to get back to Marathon. Can't afford any bad blood with my favorite barmaid."

He almost laughed. The only time Trufante was punctual was when there was alcohol involved. "Where am I going?" he asked.

FIVE

Mac followed Trufante's directions and pulled onto North Roosevelt, heading east towards Stock Island. Trufante directed him past Garrison Bight, the largest marina on the island, and they drove another quarter mile or so before pulling into the parking lot of a vanilla-looking commercial building. Mac drove slowly around back, cautious that he didn't get too close if someone was still there. Despite the reputation of chop shops as being late night businesses, he doubted there was work going on this time of night. The noise would carry and attract attention. Parked in back were several boats on trailers by a large roll-up garage door. A sign above declared the business as Custom Boats and Watersports. There were no lights or cars, so they parked, got out of the car and walked to the office door, careful to stay in the shadows of the trailered boats, in case there were surveillance cameras.

"They don't just tow these to the public ramp. It's too visible." Mac said, wondering how the operation worked.

Trufante pointed to a camouflaged gate across the parking lot that looked like it went nowhere. "That there goes back to a lagoon. You got to run the bridge at the bottom of the tide, so no one thinks you can get in or out of here. They've got a forklift inside," he pointed to the garage door. "Ain't but a hundred yards to the water. The clean boats go out the front door on trailers, the dirty ones out the back, into the lagoon, where they can disappear in the back country."

Mac slid against the building to the office door. It was solid glass, allowing him an unobstructed view of the interior. In the dim blue light from the computers he saw several desks and the usual assortment of office furniture. There was no sign of life.

"How we gonna get in?" Trufante asked.

Mac pulled the handle on the commercial-grade door, finding the deadbolt in place. He left the storefront and walked to a solid door on the other side of the garage door used to access the workspace. The steel door had a single lock and he yanked the handle, finding it locked as he expected, but it was old, and anything made out of metal in the Keys had a half-life, its useful life shortened by the weather and salty environment. A cinder block lay to the side of the door, probably used for a door stop. Mac picked up the block and raised it over his head. With a quick movement, he brought the cement block down on the handle. He felt the lock shatter, and satisfied he could get in now, he set the block back and went to work on the lock. He picked up the handle from the ground and inserted it back into the mechanism. With a few jiggles, he was able to coax the door open.

"Open the garage door," he called to Trufante and walked into the cavernous space. At least five boats were in the warehouse, many in different stages of assembly, or disassembly, in which this business specialized. None resembled Commando's boat. The two closest to the garage door looked workable. A Hydrosport 33 sat on blocks, its three 275 horsepower engines gleaming in the moonlight. A stainless steel structure lay next to it. The boat would work, but would also stand out. Although he would have liked the speed and shallow draft, the go-fast boat would be too easy to spot. The three boats in the back had no engines so he focused on the Scout. The graceful but utilitarian lines appealed to him and the twin 225 Yamaha engines were adequate power for the twenty-seven foot hull.

"Open the garage door," he repeated.

"What for?" Trufante asked.

"Change in plans. You're gonna take the car back to Annie and I'm taking a boat back to Wood's place. There's no sign of Commando's boat and I need to gear up."

"Reckon the safest place to steal a boat is from a boat thief. They ain't going to the police," Trufante said and pulled on the chain next to the door.

Mac cringed as metal creaked and the garage door went skyward, disappearing into its housing. Moonlight flooded the space. After a quick inspection of the boat, he decided it would work. The only thing he could see missing was the leaning post, but the open space in the cockpit didn't bother him, in fact it might be useful. He used the short work ladder next to the hull to climb inside. The keys were in the ignition - a relief, as he wasn't prepared to hot-wire the boat - but there was a large hole in the dashboard where the chart-plotter belonged. That was unfortunate. Newer boats used a large display with the GPS, plotter, radar and depth finder included in one unit. Some had redundant systems, but the dashboard had only the factory tachometers, oil pressure gauges for the twin engines, and a bank of switches for the navigation lights, bilge pumps, wash-downs and other small electric devices. Rather than risk the noise of dry-cranking the engines, he turned on the navigation lights. He could see the red and green light reflected from the bow. There would also be a white light on the hardtop, but for now he was satisfied the batteries were installed and charged.

"Start the lift," he called to Trufante.

The Cajun climbed into the seat of the propane-powered forklift and the engine purred. Propane lifts were cleaner and quieter than their gas counterparts and Mac was again thankful for the criminals' forethought. They also needed to get the boats in the water with little noise. He jumped down from the hull, moved the ladder out of the way, and cleared the parts and tools in the path of the lift. Trufante moved the extended forks into place under the chines and lifted the boat. Once free of the blocks, the forklift backed silently out of the space, its backup alarm thoughtfully disabled. Mac closed the garage door and ran to open the gates as Trufante swung the lift around, but they were locked. He had to run into the building again and search the office for the key. He found it on a hook by the door and ran back out to Trufante, who now had the boat facing forward, ready to roll through the opening. Mac unlocked the padlock, threw open the gate and stood back as Trufante drove the lift down the path to the water.

He moved through the brush beside the trail to get in front of the boat and saw the lagoon ahead. Another minute and Trufante had the boat extended over the water, where he lowered the hull until it was ready to float off the padded forks. Mac jumped into the boat and turned the keys. He was greeted by silence and checked the throttles, cursed, and then remembered the dead-man's switch. The hook-like keys were not engaged, defeating the starter. He fumbled with the safety mechanism, his fingers shaking, until the hooks clamped onto the posts and engaged. Again he turned the key to the starboard motor, cringing while the safety beeped, but the motor turned over and caught. He started the port engine, pulled the throttles back and reversed the boat.

"Put the lift back and leave the place like we found it," he called back to Trufante, who was already backing the lift down the trail. While he waited, he flipped switches until he found the backlights for the instrument panel and checked the fuel. The gauge showed a quarter full, but unlike cars, fuel indicators on boats were seldom accurate. There could be three quarters, or nothing in the tank. Calculating the worst case and assuming the boat held a few hundred gallons, he estimated with a quarter-tank they could make fifty miles if they didn't push too hard.

Trufante ran down the path towards him and he brought the boat forward. "Take the car. I'll meet you in Marathon in the morning."

The Cajun stopped short. "I ain't driving that road in this condition."

Mac saw the Cajun's hands shaking in the moonlight and realized he was right. He would have to take him. "Can you get the car back to the Bight." The marina was only a few blocks away and her car would blend in there. "I'll meet you there."

Mac paused, realizing he was moving too fast. With the characters involved here, the slightest misstep could get someone killed. He would have to slow down and be more careful. He checked his wrist out of habit, but the dive watch had been lost in the wreckage. With a glance at the moon, he figured it was close to one. Annie would be expecting him back in an hour. "Call her and tell her to take a cab or whatever - I'll pay her back."

Without waiting for an answer, he put the port engine in reverse and nudged the starboard throttle into forward. The boat started to spin. When it faced the bridge, Mac pushed both throttles to the idle stop and slowly motored to the skinny opening between the water and steel structure of the bridge. He glanced back. Trufante was gone. He looked up at the T-top over his head and then at the bridge above, trying to gauge whether the boat would fit. There were likely several antennae and possibly a radar bell mounted to the top, invisible from below. Without the electronic console, they were expendable. He held his breath as the boat approached the bridge. Trufante had said they brought the boats out at low tide. It was far from that now, the late summer moon bringing two and a half feet of water into the lagoon. He guessed this was not the tallest boat they'd brought through here, and with no choice, he eased the boat under the bridge. The bow fell into its shadow and the hardtop followed. He heard an antenna drag and then snap as it broke off and fell into the murky water. Another crack and the radar dome followed, but the leading edge of the hardtop was in the clear.

The boat cleared the obstacle and he pushed the throttles slightly, looking behind at the small wakes as the boat picked up speed. Mangroves blocked the opening, but he sensed where the main channel was and steered towards the area where the water seemed to be moving fastest. Branches brushed the boat as it exited the lagoon, but he knew he was in the right spot when they opened slightly, revealing clear water ahead.

Without the electronics, he had no idea how deep the water was. Finally the high tide would be to his advantage here. The lack of houses and docks lining the shore told him the water was not navigable. Just as he thought it, the lower units brushed the bottom, but his instincts automatically moved his thumb to the buttons on the side of the throttle handle. A small motor whined. He watched the engines lift from the water. He didn't expect the hull to ground, but the deep draft of the 225 HP motors was a problem. Slowly he raised the twin engines, watching the water stream from the small exit holes that showed the units were cooling as they lifted from the dark water. The stream of water continued to flow and the tips of the propellers were just visible when he released the control button and breathed out. The boat continued at an idle across the flat. He cut the wheel to the left and headed for the security of the houses on the seaward side of the Bight, the boats moored on their seawalls a sure sign there was deeper water. With the motors back down, he idled through the narrow cut and into the protection of the harbor. A quarter mile away, five docks jutted out from the seawall directly in front of him. He steered towards the middle, looking for a place to tie off and wait for Trufante.

***

Yesterday, Norm had the driver drop him at the marina just off the Palm Avenue Causeway where he had returned the rental boat after carefully cleaning any sign of the struggle with Jay. Dutifully lowering his head, he had taken the scolding from the manager about the missing antenna, the object he had used to stab his accomplice with, and gladly offered to pay for the damage. The marina was deserted now, the only signs of life were the lights coming from the cabins of a few live-aboards. He walked down the jetty to the dock where the rental boats were kept and studied each boat in the glow of the dock lights, checking the numbers on the hulls. The boat he had rented was towards the end of the row. The deckhand had instructed him to leave it at the gas dock when he returned, so he assumed it was full of fuel. He released the bowline and jumped on board, pulled the key from his bag and inserted it into the engine. There were two days remaining on the rental contract and he had insisted on keeping the keys, promising to return them before he left the island. Boats could be more useful than cars here, and with the rental paid in full, he might as well have the use of the boat.

He lowered his head after seeing a car pull up and park on the seawall. Caught full-on in the headlights, he felt like someone was staring at him. He started the engine and glanced back at the car; the silhouette of a tall man reminded him of someone, but he couldn't place him. The headlights shut off and the fifty foot distance seemed to disappear and he recognized the tall, lanky frame, long, stringy hair, and the gleam from the smile in the dock lights as the man looked right at him. With increased urgency, he went to the rear cleat, threw off the dock line, returned to the helm and backed the boat out of the slip. The man stood there staring at him and he pushed the throttle down, ignoring the idle speed signs and speeding past the line of power poles that led to the harbor exit.

SIX

Mac looked away from the unmistakable silhouette of Trufante standing on the dock to turn his attention to a rental boat coming straight at him. He turned hard to starboard to avoid the boat, staring through the dark at the driver. Once the boat passed, he idled to the middle dock and coasted to a stop. "Over here," he yelled to Trufante.

Trufante turned and ran to the boat. "It's him!" he yelled and jumped on the board. "The CIA douche from the island."

Mac didn't answer. He had already noticed the logo on the rental boats was the same as the boat that had chased him several days ago. It was too dark to see who had almost collided with him, but it was suspicious for a rental boat to be leaving in the dark of night. With no other leads, he couldn't ignore the coincidence. He pulled back on the throttles, turned the boat and followed the channel out of the harbor. The other boat had already passed the breakwater, but there was only one long channel to deep water and with no other boats, Mac knew he would be able to see where the boat went.

"What'cha doin'?" Trufante asked.

Mac had stopped by an older outboard tied up at the end of the pier. "Get their gas cans." He worked the throttles and idled next to the older boat. By its age and design, he guessed it would likely not have a permanent tank, but use portables. Worried about the fuel level in the Scout, there was no use in chasing the other boat if he ran out of gas.

Trufante sat on the gunwale waiting for Mac to close the distance between the boats. When they were within a foot, he swung his legs into the other hull and slid into the boat. Mac waited while he removed the fuel line from the first tank and lifted it. He went to the side and held the boats together while Trufante hefted the tank onto the boat. Mac set it on the deck, guessing by its weight it was near full. He slid the tank to the transom and waited while the Cajun lifted the other tank, not sure if it was full or Trufante was still drunk from the way he struggled to get it across the void and onto the boat. Mac set the second tank by the first and waited while Trufante climbed back across the gunwales before backing away from the dock and turning towards the harbor exit. The other boat would have a head start, but the Scout was faster and he could easily catch him in open water, if the need arose. For now, he was satisfied to follow at a distance.

He turned to port and followed the channel running parallel to land. The other boat was still visible further out against the backdrop of Fleming Key. "Top off the gas tank," he ordered Trufante, wanting the advantage of the protected waters and slower speed for the operation. The smell of gas wafted towards him as Trufante struggled with the heavy containers. He looked back and slowed to idle speed, giving Trufante a better chance of pouring the gas into the small hole, just large enough for the nozzle of a gas pump. The Cajun emptied the first can, tossed it aside, and started dumping the fuel from the second. Mac calculated the range of the boat while Trufante filled the tanks. With the additional twenty gallons, he figured he had another fifty miles, maybe more. If he could keep the engines in their comfort zone, they would have a range of over a hundred miles. Trufante tossed the second tank to the deck.

The other boat was around the tip of Fleming Key and out of sight. Mac inched the throttles forward. He didn't want to go too fast and spook the driver. There was only one way to go around the island and he would have eyes on him before long. There were several options once they reached the other side, but he took his time, confident the other boat would still be visible until they reached Wisteria Key and Tank Island where the deep-water channels ran from the Key West Bight. If he intended on heading east into the back country, he would likely turn into the Northwest Passage, rather than risk the unmarked waters through the flats in the dark. If he was heading further west, or around Key West to the Atlantic side, he would make his move there as well.

Mac pushed the throttles, waited for the boat to settle on plane and held the RPM's just under three thousand, the most efficient speed for the engines. At this speed he calculated they would burn around eight gallons of fuel an hour. An increase to four thousand and the consumption would be twelve gallons. The other boat was also on plane and Mac knew he needed to close the distance before he turned. The Scout crept closer to its prey. Wisteria Key passed on the port side and Tank Island came into view just ahead. The other boat was running full out, but Mac relaxed as the Scout, with its twin engines, easily closed the gap on the single outboard. He waited for the rental boat to make its move and followed after it turned to the West around Tank Island.

"What the hell?" Trufante said.

The direction concerned him. A lot of empty water and finally Cuba lay in along the course the boat was heading, but Mac knew the small rental boat was no match for the waves and current of the Gulf Stream it would have to cross before reaching Cuba – if that was its destination. He was more than likely headed to one of the islands extending from Key West towards the Dry Tortugas. What worried him was the geography of the area. Dawn would break soon, but even in the sunlight he would need electronics to navigate the shallows and shoals.

"Must be meeting someone," Mac answered. He watched the white light mounted to the T-top of the rental boat. He hit his navigation light switch and turned off his own lights. The white anchor light had been lost at the bridge, but the red and green bow lights would be visible from miles away if the man looked back. This was a desolate area, popular with fishermen and snorkelers during the day. At night they were the only boats on the water. He backed off the throttles again, bringing the boat to the slowest speed it would stay on plane. Even without navigation lights, moonlight would be enough to illuminate the boat at this range. He worked the throttle to maintain the largest gap he could and still see the white anchor light on top of the other boat.

**

Norm looked back again. He was trained to watch for vehicles tailing him. Boats were much easier to spot. He watched the outline behind him. It had been keeping its distance, but after seeing the man on the dock, he was under no illusions that he was unobserved. There was no way to outrun the larger boat, but he knew where he was going and the other boat would be forced to stay well back to avoid being seen. This was not his first rodeo and he smiled at the prospect of the chase. He glanced down at the chart-plotter that showed a small shape indicating his boat. He glanced at his phone on the dashboard; the GPS app showed distance to the waypoint ticking down and the boat's approach to the Marquesses, a small volcanic atoll where the rendezvous was to take place. It was harder to navigate with both devices rather than program the location into the rental boats unit, but tradecraft dictated caution.

The screen showed his location just off Man Key. Ballast, Woman, and Boca Grande Keys lay ahead, and then a gap of about six miles before the Marquesses. He needed to lose the boat before they reached the last stretch of open water. The chart enlarged, showing more detail of the area and he zoomed in, re-centering the display. Boca Grande Key, the largest and last land before deeper water, had a marked channel and made a good place for a clandestine meeting. From the *distance to waypoint* number, he estimated he would reach the channel just before sunrise. He focused on the chart plotter again, trying to plan a route that would lure the chase boat into thinking his destination was the back side of Boca Grande. The other boat would be able to use their electronics to follow, but they would be forced to declare themselves if they did; the area was too close to avoid visual contact. Whoever was running the other boat would have no idea if he was armed, where he was going or why. He doubted they would take the chance of a confrontation.

He glanced at the chart-plotter and focused on the cut in front of Ballast Key. From the distance the other boat was following, he hoped they would think he was entering the larger Boca Grande channel instead. Another glance behind and he saw the boat in the moonlight. They were running without lights now, clearly showing their intention to remain unseen. He laughed to himself at the amateurish move. Even the muted tones of the red and green running lights would obscure the occupants of the boat to anyone looking back on them.

At the entrance to the channel, he cut the wheel to starboard. It was his turn to go dark and he flipped off the navigation lights. He wanted the other boat to think he was blocked from view by the land mass of Boca Grande Key. He stared at the plotter, relying on the unit to show his progress as the unmarked channel would be invisible in the dark. Just past the Key he made a quick turn to port and pushed the throttle all the way down. This was his chance to escape. The boat sped past Woman Key, his eyes were glued to the depth finder. He was confident he had lost the other boat, but now the shallow water was a problem. The depth fluctuated between two and five feet, but the boat moved forward.

Ten tense minutes later, he rounded the back of Boca Grande Key and hit the deep channel. He had seen no sign of the other boat. If they were still following, he would appear to be coming from a different direction. The plotter showed him in open water. He looked at the darkness behind him. He was alone.

***

Mac pushed the throttles down hard as the boat in front turned. Without the aid of electronics, he had no choice but to follow it into the shallows. He'd been through here several times and knew the general area, but needed the plotter and depth finder to navigate the unmarked channels. The other boat was out of sight, probably behind the island in front of him. He cut the wheel and entered what he hoped was the correct channel. Suddenly he was thrown forward and lost his balance. The boat brushed the bottom again and he reached for the throttles, pulling them back hard to keep from digging any deeper. There was an old saying in boating that if you were going to hit something, hit it slow.

The boat slowed, but as it came off plane, it sank deeper into the water and stuck.

"Damn it," he muttered. The chase was over. It would be hours before the tide brought enough water to lift them off the bottom.

***

Norm slowed at the cut leading into Mooney Harbor in the center of the Marquesas Keys. White mast lights and the faint outlines of several boats anchored in the protected water were just visible. He entered the channel and steered towards the shore of the largest island following its jagged shape, using the plotter to keep him in deep water until he reached the tip. The GPS beeped. He looked up and saw a large trawler anchored several hundred yards ahead. Breathing deeply, he tried to settle his mind after the chase. He would need all his wits for this meeting.

At idle speed he closed the distance and saw the outline of three figures on the other boat. He thought two looked like they were uniformed and he tensed as the boats came together. Norm caught the line one of the men tossed to him and tied it to a cleat. The boats coasted to within a few feet and the other man tossed a bumper over the side and pulled them together. Norm got a good look at the men. He was right about the uniforms, but his heart missed a beat - they were Cuban.

He had a quick moment of panic where he wanted to release the line and get out of there. Despite the risk, when the third man rose, his curiosity piqued. The figure, still in the shadow of the cabin, was also in uniform, his pock-marked face was illuminated when he pulled on his cigar.

"Generalissimo," Norm called across the boats.

SEVEN

Another fifteen minutes and they would have been able to see the muck they were stuck in, Mac thought as he stared at the dark brown bottom surrounding them. The sun's rays pierced the surface now and clearly showed the bottom.

"Now what we gonna do?" Trufante asked.

Mac looked over at the Cajun, sitting on the deck as if he were ready for a nap. "What do you think we're going to do. I'm not waiting on the tide." He looked around the boat again. The turtle grass waving in the current below them was not a good sign. Had they grounded in sand, the water would have been a light, almost clear green and they could have pushed the boat off the harder bottom. Turtle grass meant mud, the kind of bottom that would trap you to the knee like quicksand and create a powerful suction on the hull.

"Can you hold off on the nap for a while; I know you've had a few rough days with the party and all, but I need you to keep watch. That rental boat's range is limited. I expect he'll come back this way," Mac said.

Trufante had propped himself up on the gunwale, his head resting in his arms. He looked like he'd be asleep in minutes.

Mac shielded his eyes, squinted into the rising sun, and cursed his luck. The CIA man was out there somewhere, and if he could figure out what he was doing, it might give him the leverage he needed to clear his name and help Mel. He inspected the water around the stuck hull, anxious to free the boat before the man returned. Although they had lost him, the channel had an unimpeded view of any boats passing by. The wind was down, the seas calm, and the tourists were already starting to take advantage of another beautiful day in paradise. With the additional boat traffic, it wouldn't be nearly as hard or risky to follow him.

He went forward, opened the hatch where the anchor was stored, and grinned at the Fortress anchor in the hold. The rest of the boat had been stripped down by the chop shop, even life jackets and flares, the rudimentary safety equipment the Coast Guard required had been removed. Finding an anchor at all was a stroke of luck, and especially the Fortress; the lightweight aluminum anchor would bury in the mud, unlike the grapnels many Keys boats used for anchors. The two empty gas cans were the only other objects he had to work with. He started forming a plan.

"Hey. Wake up!" he called to Trufante, whose head rolled to the side.

He turned a bloodshot eye to Mac. "Yo."

"In the water," Mac ordered.

"In that crap?" Trufante responded slowly and looked over the side.

Mac glared back and waited while Trufante slowly gained his feet and stripped off his shirt. "Take the empty cans with you."

Trufante leapt in the water, a can in each hand. Mac directed him to set one under each side, just behind the V shaped bow where the hull flattened out. The boat would need to come off backwards and he wanted the lift from the tanks to break the suction of the mud. He came close to jumping in to help, but Trufante finally managed to wrestle the buoyant tanks under the boat. Their effect was unnoticeable.

The Cajun looked back up at him, panting from the exertion. "Ain't doin' squat."

Mac ignored him and went forward to the anchor compartment where he lifted the lightweight anchor from the hold and set the ten feet of chain gently on the deck.

"Now swim this out past the stern."

He started tossing line towards Trufante who waded towards him and took the anchor. The lanky figure lunged through the mud in a kind of half-swim half-walk. He looked like he was tiptoeing, fighting hard to escape the embrace of the muck. With a standard anchor, he would have sunk, but with the lightweight Fortress over his shoulder he moved past the boat. Mac paid out the line until it reached the bitter end and called for Trufante to drop the anchor. It disappeared into the muck and he secured the line to a cleat while Trufante swam back to the boat. Mac waited until he was back aboard before he started pulling on the rope in quick, hard jerks to set the flukes. The line came tight and, satisfied it was secure, he called for Trufante. The two men strained to pull the boat free from the grasp of the mud. With all they had, they heaved on the line, but to no avail. Mac had hoped the empty gas tanks would allow the boat to slide and their buoyancy would help break the suction but the hull remained glued to the bottom.

"You got to check the cans again. Make sure they aren't stuck too."

Trufante looked done, but he needed him in the water.

"Do this and I'll let you sleep on the way back."

Mac watched as Trufante breathed in several breaths and then disappeared into the dark water. He made several trips down before he climbed back aboard. "Should be good now."

Mac went to the helm and pushed the button to raise the engines. He wanted to make sure they were clear of the water. He thought about using their power to help pull them off, but decided against it. Pulling by hand, although harder, let him feel their progress. One burst from the engines could grind them deeper into the mud - deep enough that even the tide couldn't help.

Both men were standing in the cockpit with the line in their hands.

"Pull," Mac called out, and their muscles stained as they struggled to gain line. They tried twice more without bringing in even an inch. What they needed was mechanical advantage and Mac looked around the bare boat for anything that could help. A block and tackle were the tools he needed, but the boat didn't even have a windlass for the anchor. He looked at the engines, the stainless steel blades of the propellers glistening in the sun, and had an idea.

He took the line from the cleat and brought the end over to the port engine. If they'd had a single engine, he never would have tried this, but with two, it was worth the risk. They could sacrifice one if it got them out of the mud. He took the line, wrapped it around the propeller shaft and went to the helm, where he lowered the engine until the intake was barely submerged. The engine started and he called for Trufante to stay clear of the line. With the lightest touch he had, he pushed the throttle forward. The propeller shaft spun, but didn't grab. Mac goosed the throttle and the motor started to stall as the line caught. As it came tight he pushed harder. Drops of water flew from the fibers of the rope, the tension increasing until finally, the boat jerked. He breathed deeply and pushed a little further.

"Shit, its working," Trufante yelled.

Mac ignored him. They were not free yet. He checked the propeller and saw the line neatly wound around the shaft. As long as it didn't start to wrap on the blades, he could pull more. Two things could happen if the line caught the blades, and both were bad. Either the line would be sliced by the sharp propeller or the blade would be bent, disabling the entire engine.

"Watch the line on the blades," he called to Trufante. Once more he pushed the throttle and the line jerked. He pursed his lips and gave it a little more power. The engine sounded like it was ready to stall again. He was just about to back off when the boat shifted. With a quick push forward, it moved again. Finally the gas cans had done their job and were floating in front of the boat. He shut down the port engine, lowered and started the starboard one, and pulled the throttle back into reverse.

"Take in the slack," he said to Trufante, who stood behind him watching. He didn't want the line stretched behind the boat to entangle the other propeller.

The boat slid backwards as Trufante pulled in the line.

"Secure it," Mac ordered.

Trufante went forward and tied off the anchor. The boat swung around with the current, unimpeded by the bottom. Mac went back examining the shaft as the line unwrapped from the port engine. It looked OK, but he wouldn't know for sure until he ran it. Even the slightest deformity would cause the shaft to spin out of true and trash the lower unit.

***

Norm accepted the cigar and sat in the deck chair next to the small man, whose pockmarked face was visible even with the cover of his beard.

"You have something that belongs to me?" the general asked in a tone of voice that told Norm he already knew the answer.

A cloud of smoke hid Norm's face as he thought about the implications of what the man said. He had been at this game for years and had many things that belonged to many people; specific to Cuba was the string of baseball players he had smuggled out of the island. Surprised his operation had caught the attention of a high ranking official, especially one of the old guard like General Choy, he looked blankly at the man. For years he had been smuggling younger players with promise, taking a chance on their talent. He carefully avoided the big-time players that would attract the attention of the regime. Once they were in the US, his business plan was to falsify the players' identities and get them minor league tryouts. About half made it; the ones that did owed him ten percent of their earnings for life. Over the years he had many wash out, but a few big hits had enlarged his offshore bank account.

He decided to play along. "And what might that be?"

"Please don't play us for fools. We know what you've been doing. Very smart, really," he said, and blew a smoke ring towards Norm.

"So why not stop me?" Norm asked.

"The players were of no consequence. If you had gone after bigger names we would, of course, have been forced to put you out of business, but the men you chose had no risk of embarrassing us. We chose to sit back and watch, especially your rise within the organization." He paused and blew another smoke ring. "Very impressive. You Americans are not known for your patience."

It was all out in the open now and Norm needed to find out what they wanted from him. "And how may I be of service to you?"

The general smiled, taking the bait. "I don't expect your government will appreciate what you have done like we do. You could make a case for helping political refugees escape our tyrannical government, but there is the matter of the money. I can see you sitting in front of one of those witch hunts your press calls Congressional investigation panels. Those grandstanding politicians will be waiting in line for a piece of your hide."

Norm looked down, no longer interested in either the conversation or the cigar. He just wanted to find out what they wanted from him and to get out of there. "So, general…"

The general paused again, chewing on, trimming, and then relighting the cigar. This was clearly a tactic to annoy Norm, and he should have known it for what it was, but instead he pushed. "What do you want from me?"

"My grandson, Armando Cruz."

The name took him by surprise. He knew he had made a mistake and also knew there would be no negotiation.

"You have two days. The inaugural voyage of the Key West to Havana ferry leaves then. There are many people - some high up in the Cuban Government - that are against these new relations between our countries. I am one of them, but am willing to sacrifice the cause to get my grandson back. You deliver him to me and the boat will make its voyage."

The threat was clear.

EIGHT

"Where is he?" One of the men leaned forward and checked his watch. "Jules would have been here on time. She had a lot more respect than this new sheriff."

The five heads comprising the ethics committee appeared to nod, but not one lifted their head from the screen of their phones. The blinds were closed to keep the morning sun out, the group happy to trade comfort for the view of Boot Key Harbor.

"I have surgery in an hour," a woman chimed in. "Can we get started? He doesn't need all the details."

"Probably wouldn't understand anyway," another voice added.

The man at the head of the table opened a folder, lifted a page and started reading aloud. "Patient is Melanie Woodson: admitted by medevac approximately forty-eight hours ago. Patient had severe head trauma and water in her lungs after surviving a boating accident." He thumbed through several more pages. "The latest prognosis is bad. She has been unresponsive and in a coma since she got here, and she meets several of the criteria for brain death."

"Insurance?"

"We located a Blue Cross account through a computer search. They have a rep coming down from Miami now."

The hospital administrator tried to hide her smile with the revelation that at least the hospital would not be on the hook for the cost of the medical care.

"Next of kin or living will?" someone asked.

"The only family I know of was her dad, Bill Woodson. Wood lost his wife several years ago. He is deceased as well."

The group was silent for a minute as they remembered how Wood had died exposing a corrupt presidential candidate and saving South Florida from a nuclear blast.

The man cleared his throat, clearly growing impatient. "Does anyone know anything? And where is that sheriff?"

"I knew her dad pretty well, used to fish with him," one of the doctors said. "He built the dock on my house too." Eyes turned to him and he handed a piece of paper to the man at the head of the table. "She used to work for Bradley Davies in DC. I called the firm and they sent this over. It appears to be the only document they have."

The man took the paper and started reading. Just as he was about to speak, the door burst open and a heavy man in a tight-fitting uniform entered. He mumbled something and went to an empty seat, his coffee spilling as he sat.

"Good afternoon, Sheriff," the doctor said.

The sheriff looked at his watch. "Still morning by my clock."

The others suppressed giggles as the sheriff missed the barb.

The man stopped reading and looked up. "OK. The first decision maker was her dad, now deceased. The next is Mac Travis, currently missing by the last reports I heard. I'm not sure how long until he is assumed dead."

All eyes turned to the sheriff.

He cleared his throat. "Ms. Woodson and the Cuban fellow were rescued. We haven't found any sign of Travis, although we'd surely like to beat the feds - dead or alive, makes no difference to me." His radio squelched causing several in the group to jump. "Y'all got any food at these meetings," he asked after turning his radio off, dismissing the call.

The head man ignored him. "After Travis, the executor of the will is Bradley Davies."

"That old boy's shacked up in some country club prison in Virginia." The sheriff said.

A new voice chimed in, "Is there any precedence in a convict making medical decisions?"

The room was quiet for a minute. "Yes," the administrator said. "If that's all we have, I suggest we contact him."

The leader closed the file and turned to the man who had handed him the paper. "OK, you contact Davies." He turned to the sheriff, his look clearly contemptuous, "And you find Travis. We will meet again after the insurance rep gets here."

***

Mac moved the anchor line to the bow cleat, fighting as the boat spun against the strong current until it was tied off. The tidal force sounded like a river as it moved against the stationary hull, but they were secure. They were less mobile to pursue the CIA man with the hook set, but the current in the narrow cut forced his hand. Under power, they would burn precious fuel, fighting the current to remain in the center of the cut. He looked over at Trufante's prone body laid out on the deck, asleep.

Might as well let him get some rest, Mac thought.

He had no idea how long the watch would last, or if the man would even come back this way, but it was the only card he had left.

He thought about Mel in the hospital and hoped she was all right, but as much as he wanted to be there, he knew there was nothing he could do until he cleared himself. The only thing he had left was his name, and right now it was as mucky as the bottom underneath the boat. He looked up as several fish jumped pursuing a school of baitfish past the boat. It had been a half hour since they had freed the boat and several boats had passed at a distance, including some bigger charter boats probably heading for Fort Jefferson in the Dry Tortugas. He wondered where Norm could have gone - and why. The rental boat didn't have the range to get to the Tortugas and back. The only thing that made sense was some kind of clandestine meeting, and he thought the Marquesas Keys would be the likely place for that.

His head bobbed as sleep tried to take him, but the wake of a passing boat snapped his neck erect. This was starting to feel pointless, sitting here. If the man chose to return even a mile further offshore, he would be invisible without binoculars. Maybe heading back to Key West and scouring the bars would be more productive. Either way, finding the man was going to be like catching a single minnow in the ocean. He started the engines and went to the bow to release the anchor. Trufante stirred and he thought about waking him on the way back to the helm, but he remembered his promise to let him sleep.

Hand over hand, he pulled the boat closer to the anchor until the line was perpendicular and the hull was right over it. With a quick jerk he yanked the hook from the bottom and brought it aboard, careful to dip it several times to clear the muck from the flukes and chain. Once secured, he moved back to the helm where he corrected the drift and steered the boat back into the middle of the channel. Something glimmered in the distance - the unmistakable shine of sun on bright metal - what he guessed was a quarter-mile offshore. He shielded his eyes from the sun, once again wishing for binoculars, and studied the outline of the boat. Without hesitation he pushed down on the throttles and sped out of the cut.

***

Bradley Davies sat in front of the warden, working hard to conceal the smirk on his face. Aside from the orange jumpsuit and the two-star rating he would give the kitchen, his stay here had been anything but hard. Female companionship was even scheduled after he faked a marriage license with a call girl and petitioned a judge he knew for conjugal visits. He was living large on the government's dime. Gardening and tennis had to substitute for golf. His trimmer waistline was the only benefit of his forced lifestyle. He sighed.

"Someone actually left you as executor on their will?" the warden asked.

If not for his years of putting on a game face in front of juries, he would have laughed out loud. "Why the hate? You don't need a license for that. And some people trust my judgement."

He had been the head of one of the biggest firms in DC, before his fall from grace after it was revealed, partially through Mel's efforts, that some old terrorist clients had blackmailed him into setting up the President for an assassination attempt. Near the end of his first year at the old country club, as his fellow inmates called it, he was ready for a divorce and getting fidgety for the comforts of the outside world. He often wondered how he would survive the hardships of the remaining four years of his sentence.

The warden knew Davies had the upper hand although he tried to humble him with his patented look over his reading glasses.

"Oh, stop it. You know as well as I do that this is a game and I just got dealt a winning hand." More than anything else with prison life, it infuriated him that he was controlled by men so inferior to him.

The warden stared at him as if he knew what was coming.

"Of course, I'll need to travel to Marathon to see the condition of the girl first-hand. This is a grave matter and must be handled in person." This was so easy he had to steel his face again. "I wouldn't be able to live with myself if I didn't do my due diligence."

"Get a judge to sign it and I'll work out the details," the warden said and rose.

The meeting was over. Davies got up fighting the urge to extend his hand. Surly as he was, he still needed the warden to be his pawn, and although it tore him apart, he had to show the man respect. He turned and walked to the door, where a guard waited to take him to his tennis match.

***

The hull smashed through the wake again, causing Mac to duck behind the windscreen. Instinctively he turned his head to avoid the spray and watched the sea water covering Trufante who stirred and sat up. Mac turned back to the bow, found the rental boat, and made a correction to their course until the other boat appeared to remain in place on the horizon.

"You're on a collision course," Trufante said. He shook out his hair and ducked behind the windscreen beside Mac.

Mac's fingers tightened on the wheel. "I'm tired of chasing him. I think it's time we had a face-to-face."

"Shit, that's a roll of the dice, and being CIA and all, he's bound to have them rigged."

"Got no choice." He focused on the chase. He estimated they would be on him in five minutes. He watched the gap close and steered straight for the other boat. Talking points swirled around his mind. Provided he could signal the man that he wanted to talk, and didn't get them both shot, he needed a very persuasive argument to force the man to do what he needed. He had little to offer other than his silence, and Armando, but he knew the man could easily kill them, dump their bodies in the ocean, and find the Cuban on his own. That would be ironic, Mac thought, as he was already assumed drowned.

He adjusted course to put him slightly in front of the other boat and pushed down the throttles to the stops. He needed to use the speed of the boat to his advantage to throw the other man off guard. They closed to within a quarter mile and watched. The man realized what was happening and tried to turn behind them. Mac countered and the gap closed to two hundred yards. He could clearly see the man reach behind his back and pull a gun. They were a hundred yards away and he saw the man flinch with only a split second to make his decision. Mac steered wide and circled the boat. The other boat slowed and the man lowered the weapon.

Mac dropped the speed to an idle and coasted to a stop in front of the rental boat. He stayed behind the windscreen, hoping its tempered glass would stop the bullet he thought was coming, and raised his hands. "Just want to talk," he yelled over the engines. "Gonna throw a line over."

Trufante tossed a line to the man while Mac maneuvered the boat alongside. The man put the gun in his waistband, caught the line and tied it off to a cleat. Both men put their engines in neutral, neither willing to shut them off, and went to the adjacent gunwales.

"What can I do for you?" the man called across the gap.

Mac stuttered, his rehearsed lines fading from memory. "Let's end this. I got no war with you."

The man stared back, clearly more comfortable in this kind of situation. "Relax, Travis. You need me more than you know."

NINE

Mac followed the rental boat into the channel between Man and Crawfish Keys, careful to follow in the wake of the other boat. He had already experienced what could happen without a GPS and depth finder in these waters.

Norm was arrogant enough that he didn't even look back to see if they were still behind him. He knew Mac was like a gut-hooked fish and there was no place else to get help.

It went against Mac's grain to deal with people he knew he couldn't trust, but desperation makes people do things they wouldn't ordinarily do.

The other boat reached the backside of a mangrove-covered island and dropped anchor. Mac idled over and they tied the boats together.

The men faced off, each standing by the gunwale of their boats, neither willing to share the same deck.

"Why the look, Travis," Norm said. "It's not like you have anywhere else to turn. I hear your girl's in the hospital too."

"Leave her out of this," Mac growled.

"Suit yourself. Just saying it might be nice to be able to visit."

"Let's hear it. I need my name cleared and I'm thinking you're the fastest way to get that done," he said with his head down, fumbling with the lines that held the boats together and thinking about the tenuous tie between them. There had to be something the CIA man wanted from him if he was willing to help. "Bait's in the water. You wouldn't be sitting here if you didn't need me for something - so spit it out."

The other man thought for a minute. Mac held the lines tighter as if clinging to his best hope.

"Truth, Travis, I like your style. No screwing around." He paused. "You get me the Cuban out of the Krome. You know that place up in Miami, used to be called a detention center, now they've got on the politically correct bandwagon and call it a processing center. Anyway, you do that for me and I'll see what I can do for you."

"You can do that with one phone call," Mac said.

"If it was only so easy; you see, the Cubans want him back."

Mac suspected there was something else. "That can't be all of it. With your connections …"

"You want my help or not, Travis? I'm losing patience here." His voice rose and he paused. "The man trusts you, and with all the publicity about the new diplomatic and trade relations with old Raul, it wouldn't look good for the media to get a hold of a story like this."

Mac tried to process this and run it through his BS detector. He'd been around the transients that passed through the Keys for years, each bringing their own story of how the world had wronged them. Trufante was a prime example, as his own past changed with each telling and the number of beers he had. This had a ring of truth to it, and that small nugget was enough to hold Mac's interest. And the man was right. Armando might trust him.

"So I get him out of Krome and bring him to you - that's it?"

"Almost; you need to repatriate him."

"Repatriate what?" Mac heard Trufante mumble behind him.

He ignored him. Something was not right here. Once Mac had the man, he had all the cards. He could hide him somewhere, leaving the CIA man powerless. Then he realized they would be at a stalemate. There had to be some leverage here, he thought.

"Deal, but I'm going to need some official papers or ID to get him out of Krome." The processing center resembled a jail and in fact, the old name might have been more accurate.

"I've got an associate that can help you out. You got a phone?" Norm asked.

"Lost it somewhere in the wreck," Mac answered and flinched as the man reached into his bag, but what he thought was the black handle of a gun turned into a phone.

"It's a burner. When we're done, destroy it. My number is programmed into it. As soon as we get back to Key West, I'll set things up on my end. Be expecting a call tonight," he said and tossed Mac the phone.

"Tell me what time and I'll have it on," Mac said, looking the plain black, old-style flip phone over. He suspected at the least it had some kind of tracking device in it, maybe even a camera or listening device. He would remove the battery once the other boat was out of sight.

"Seven," Norm responded.

Mac grunted and started to release the lines. "We done?" he asked as the boats moved apart.

"Just remember - you need me. Don't screw this up."

Mac turned to Trufante and handed him the phone. "Take out the battery." He followed the wake of the rental boat until he saw the water change color to a dark blue, deep enough that he no longer needed his escort. He turned seaward and pushed down the throttle. The boat jumped forward, and crashed through the waves, Mac using the wheel to balance as well as steer. The pounding of the hull against the seas felt good - water under him, spray flying around them, and just the plain speed uncluttered his head. He looked over at Trufante, who held a stainless steel rail anchored to the dashboard; the grille that was his smile glittered in the sunlight.

Key West came into view and he changed course slightly, scanning the horizon for the first green channel marker. It appeared a minute later and he kept the boat straight, lining up the more distant markers behind it. He passed the last pile, turned to port and entered the channel. They entered the space between Tank Island, the old military depot, now the tourist haven called Sunset Key, and the mainland when he saw the boat coming straight towards them.

"That's Commando's old hull," Mac yelled to Trufante. "Missing the top, but I can tell from here."

"Shit!" Trufante said. "Boys must be on the prowl looking for us."

Mac had taken the Scout and not one of the more distinctive go-fast boats to blend in better, but in the close quarters of the channel there was nowhere to turn. They couldn't outrun the faster boat. He pulled back on the throttle to buy some more time and desperately searched for a way out. The boat was closing fast and he felt something wiz by his head. A second later he heard the retort and ducked. Instinctively he swerved the boat to disrupt their aim, but the next shot hit the windshield, shattering it into tiny pieces. The tempered glass held, but his view was obstructed and he was forced to lean out of its protection to see.

They were just about to pass the cruise ship pier when a line of jet skis appeared from its bow. Another bullet hit the console and he steered towards the convoy, hoping the men would not shoot at tourists. The lead jet ski slowed, waiting for the rest of the pack, before angling his craft and gunning it towards Sunset Key. Mac wondered about the safety of the maneuver, but jet skiers had a reputation for ignoring the rules of the road and doing whatever they wanted. The others followed and Mac used the diversion to cut behind them.

The line of jet skis extended across the channel, disrupting traffic and causing both boats to slow. Mac needed to keep the tourist train between them as a buffer until he could figure something out. Just as he was about to accelerate behind them, two stragglers appeared and he got an idea. He cut the wheel hard to starboard and angled the boat to force the two skiers back in the small harbor behind the cruise ship. The jet skis had no choice but to stop and seek shelter behind the liner. Mac spun the wheel and steered between the bow and seawall, almost crashing as the hull slid into the turn. He looked behind to see if he was being followed, but the only thing visible was the mass of the ship, tourists leaning over the rails.

Mac looked around the small harbor. The five docks jutting out from the seawall were all crowded with launches shuttling passengers to experience Key West for the day. He turned to look at the ship and saw a string of jet skis tied off to the landing where cruisers disembarked for shore excursions. A portable dock jutted from the boat, impatient tourists massed at the gate waiting for a launch to return to take them to the shopping and decadence of Duval Street.

They had to act fast. Mac cut the wheel, and pulled back on the throttles, allowing the boat to coast to the side of the landing. Men and women, uniformed to look like naval officers, called out to him to keep clear, but he knew the bars on their epaulets held no authority. Several held radios to their heads, probably calling security.

"We have to ditch the boat and lose them on the ship," Mac yelled to Trufante. The boat slammed into the metal landing. Mac jumped onto the retractable dock, pushed past two men holding clipboards and forced his way into the mass of tourists. He heard screams as the visitors moved out of the way. They had seconds to find a hiding spot on the cruise ship before security found them.

Trufante was behind him as they exited the mass of people waiting their turn to go ashore and ran past the shore excursion desk, where he overheard a rotund tourist repeat his room number to the befuddled agent. He looked left, but saw only shops surrounding the huge atrium in the lobby. The area was too exposed. To the right was a hallway with cabin doors on each side. A chime startled him as he passed the elevator on the starboard side and they ran back to the restrooms.

Mac entered the marble-lined bathroom, cracked the door and watched the hallway. A toilet flushed and he jumped, but it was only Trufante playing with the expensive fixtures. Three men ran from the elevator, past the bathrooms, in the direction of the excursion desk.

"You done playing?" He looked back at the Cajun fixing his hair in the mirror. Without waiting for an answer, he left the cover of the bathroom and ran for the open elevator door. It started to close before Trufante reached him and the Cajun stalled in the opening, but the doors reopened. Mac grabbed him and pulled him into the mirror-lined cab. He pushed the button and the two men were left alone in the compartment.

"Twelve freakin' stories," Trufante said. He started to push the button for deck twelve. "Crap, Mac, you could live on this sucker." He grabbed the rail as the elevator took off. "Wonder what they have for bars? I could use a cocktail right about now."

Mac felt a queasy feeling in his stomach and tried to remember the last time he was in an elevator. He could take ten-foot seas, but this floating den of iniquity was too much for him. Trufante was looking at a pamphlet he had picked up from the floor.

"What in the world? They got a rock wall on a ship." He stared at the brochure. "Damn, Mac, pools and shit too."

Mac grabbed it from him and hit the button for deck eight, remembering the room number of the tourist at the desk. The map in the brochure showed staterooms lining both sides of the boat. What they needed was a place to hide, not a pool to lounge in. The elevator beeped and the doors opened. A maid cart caught his attention and he looked to the left. He fought the urge to run and walked casually towards it.

"Wait here," he told Trufante. "Room 8012. After she lets me in, make sure you give it some time, and then come down." He pushed the lanky giant into a small alcove and continued towards the cart. The sound of a vacuum came from an open door. He peered into the room. "Ma'am," he called to the maid. "My wife went ashore and took the key. Would you mind letting me into our room?"

She shut off the vacuum and gave him a quick look. He knew he looked bad. "Kind of had too much to drink last night and we got in a fight."

She nodded and pulled a card from a retractable holder on her belt. "What room?"

He didn't expect any problems from her. It wasn't like you could just walk onto the ship. "8012," he said, hoping she had already cleaned that room, and held his breath as she walked towards the door and swiped her card in the lock.

"Thank you. I really appreciate it," he said. He pulled the do not disturb card from the back of the door and placed it on the handle. "I've got to sleep this off." He winked at her. "Don't worry about this room today." He closed the door and waited for the vacuum to start. It started again and he propped the door open and waved to Trufante.

The bulk of the two men made what was advertised as a luxurious cabin feel cramped. Trufante was looking in drawers and pawing through the luggage. "We've got some time. Let's get cleaned up and figure out what to do," Mac said and went to the bathroom.

"Wonder what kind of umbrella drinks they serve. Seems like the right kind of place for some froufrou." Trufante grinned.

TEN

Bradley Davies leaned forward in the small cubicle and studied the documents in front of him. Even though he had practically memorized it, he read Mel's living will again, trying to twist the words to his goals, making notes on the legal pad. This was the perfect opportunity - one he never thought he would have - to silence her. Once his student, her fiery personality and steamroller vision had helped him in his causes. She was a tool though, and never saw the back deals that lined his pockets, at least until she started hanging around that guy in the Keys. Now she was a liability, the one person that knew all the skeletons in his closet. Her view of justice was different than his, and she had apparently been placated when he was sentenced. His view had a more permanent tone to it.

He set the will aside and started another list with what he would need once he was released. Any minute now, he expected the papers to come through.

Another prisoner came towards him. "Warden wants you."

Davies stacked the papers and pad together, placed them under his arm, and followed the man back to the warden's office. He waited outside, smiling at the secretary until called in. It was a game he played, a kind of primitive flirting, as he watched her fidget under his unwavering smile. If you stared at someone with a scowl on your face, they would likely turn away, but smiles made people react differently and he watched her constantly shifting to glance back at him. He guessed she didn't get smiled at too often.

The door opened and the game ended. "You must still have friends in high places," the warden said.

Davies didn't respond. The warden had a piece of paper in his hand and he knew he was going to paradise. No point blowing it with a smart-ass comment.

"Sue," he handed her the paper, "please get a guard to escort him." He turned back to Davies. "I wouldn't trust you to make medical decisions about my goldfish," he said and turned back to his office. "A Federal Marshall will escort you to the sheriff in Monroe County, who will handle it from there."

Davies took a seat and resumed the game while he waited. Things were moving well and with any luck he would be in Marathon tonight. A guard entered the room and the secretary handed him a paper with his instructions. He looked at Davies, who rose, and they walked towards the intake area of the facility. Davies was handed a bag with his possessions and another guard pointed to a restroom.

The suit hung off him, at least a size too big now, but the expensive fabric felt good. He walked to the mirror and tied the silk tie, a little surprised that his hands remembered the movement. He deemed himself presentable and left the room. A man in a much cheaper suit was waiting by the guards' desk. He looked up at Davies and without a word, signed the paper the guard pushed towards him.

"Hold out your hands," the Marshall said, reached behind his back and dangled a pair of handcuffs which he laced around Davies' wrists, a little tighter than he would have liked. Together they walked out the door into the afternoon sunshine. A curious onlooker might have wondered why they were both smiling. He clutched the legal pad and folder under his arm, enjoying the feel of the suit and the Italian leather on his feet as he walked to the waiting car.

Davies held his head high and the Marshall opened the passenger door for him, got into the driver's seat and started the car. A few minutes later he looked behind him at the prison receding in the landscape. He sat back, hoping if everything went right this would be the last time he saw it.

***

"I called in to see what time the ship leaves. Figured I'd get some room service." Trufante sat on the bed watching TV, eating a giant burger and sipping a beer when Mac emerged from the steaming bathroom. "Got one for you too," he said.

Mac went to the table, lifted the lid on the plate and took several large bites.

"About time you did something useful." He took another bite. "Don't suppose you got a beer for me?" He already knew the answer when he saw the empty bottle on the floor.

"Ship pulls out of here at six tonight. The launches are due back at five."

Mac finished the burger. It wouldn't be a bad idea to get a few hours' sleep on a real bed, and maybe some more food. The chop shop guys had probably recovered the boat and were placated, at least for now. The ship's security detail would be looking for them, but he expected them to confine the search to the public areas. A room-to-room search would alarm too many people. As long as the occupants of this stateroom were living large in Key West, there was no reason to leave.

He stretched out on the twin bed and tried to sleep, but the wreck replayed in his mind again. The last thing he heard before he drifted off was Mel scream as she and Armando entered the life raft.

***

Norm pulled up to the rental dock and tossed a line to the waiting attendant. Without a word he handed him a five-dollar bill and walked towards the seawall. A lot had happened this morning and he needed a meal and somewhere to sit and think to work things out. He walked towards a cab parked by the marina office and opened the back door, waking the driver in the process.

"Duval Street," he told the man.

The driver shook the cobwebs from his dreadlocks. "Where be, mon?" the driver asked with a heavy accent.

"Hog's Breath," Norm answered, trying to ignore the smell of weed.

The cab pulled off the curb, nearly hitting a bicycle, and swerved into traffic. Horns blared as the driver navigated the mixture of bikes, scooters, pedestrians and cars, many ignoring the sidewalks and lanes. The cab turned left on Eaton and a dozen blocks later, pulled to a stop just short of Duval Street

"You can walk faster than I can drive you from here, mon," the driver said and told him the fare.

Norm dug in his pocket and pulled out a ten, handing it to the driver and waving off the change. He needed to get out of the cab whatever the cost. He walked to Duval and turned right. Past Caroline and Greene streets, he saw the sign for The Hog's Breath Saloon, but decided against it and passed by, walking another block to a short flight of stairs leading to Teasers. He always thought better in the dark.

He paid the bouncer the five-dollar cover and walked into the cave-like club. There were several stages with girls gyrating in different phases of undress. The club was near empty, but there were a few tables and stools occupied. He sat at the bar and ordered a beer. The blonde on stage caught his attention and he wondered if she could play the part he had in mind. With the beer in hand, he walked over to the padded rail and took a seat. She came over and squatted, her crotch at eye level. He leaned forward, stuck a hundred in her waiting garter, and as she bent over, he asked to speak to her privately.

She glanced around the room. Norm knew this could go either way. She was either going to turn him in for trying to solicit her, or make sure no one was watching and take him up on his offer. He followed her gaze to the bouncer, reading a newspaper by the door, and then to the bartender, who was busy stocking beer bottles into a cooler.

"I get off at six. You meet me here." She whispered an address in his ear. "And bring a few more of your friends."

He nodded and walked back to the bar to keep an eye on her, not interested in her moves now, but more in her interactions. He had a few hours to judge whether she was right for what he had in mind. Worst case, he was out a hundred and got a good show; best case, she would fit his job description.

After the second beer, his attention started to wander. There was only so much ass you could watch without touching, he felt. The conversation with the generalissimo took over his thoughts and he tried to figure out a way to make the Cuban's demands work to his advantage. The novelty of the bar had worn off and his mind was wandering, He finished his beer, paid the bartender, leaving a generous tip, and went for the door. The girl gave a quick wink, which he returned with an almost imperceptible nod, confirming their rendezvous. He left the cold, dark room behind and went down the stairs, his exposed skin instantly crawling with beads of sweat when it met the humid air.

He walked down the street and entered a small electronics store where he paid cash for two pre-paid cell phones. He had given his last one to Travis, and in this business they were invaluable. The open air patio of a small bistro just off Duval caught his eye and he wandered over and took a table. After ordering, he opened one of the packages, checked the contacts in his phone and entered a number in the burner.

A woman who sounded more like a teenage girl answered.

"If you are still interested in getting some field experience, I may have a job for you."

***

Davies walked down the narrow stairs leading from the plane to the steamy tarmac of Key West Airport and smiled. More a fan of an air-conditioned office, he was never so happy to be bathed in humidity. The Marshall followed him down the stairs and motioned him to stay within the cones and follow the airline employee leading the passengers into the building. They walked straight through the terminal, the Marshall carrying a briefcase that was too expensive for his suit. Davies clutched the legal pad and folder tightly under his arm and they entered a waiting car.

"Pull out and drive around the airport," the Marshall instructed the driver.

Davies looked over at him and held out his hands. The man removed the handcuffs and handed him the briefcase. They were almost at the exit and Davies instructed the driver to go to the departing passengers' area of the terminal. He waited until they were at the curb and nodded as the Marshall exited the car. He watched him look both ways and enter the terminal. Once he was sure he was gone, Davies instructed the driver to head towards Marathon. They left the airport and the car turned north on US 1. He looked out the window. One more step and he was a free man, but he had work to do before he could enjoy his freedom. The cost to bribe the judge and set up the fake Marshall had severely drained his off-shore account and there was still one Melanie Woodson to take care of.

The car turned right onto the Stock Island Bridge and he looked down at the briefcase. He spun the lock to his birth date and held his breath as the clasp released. Inside he found a passport with his likeness and another name, two credit cards, a Texas driver's license, a cell phone, and an envelope full of cash. With his escape kit in hand, he put the legal pad and folder inside, closed his eyes and dreamed of his future.

ELEVEN

Mac slowly opened his eyes. It was still daylight, but he could tell it was late afternoon by the shadow cast across the cabin window. The bed underneath him felt good and he had to fight the urge to close his eyes again. A knock on the door startled him awake. Trufante went to answer.

"What are you doing?" he asked.

"Just needed some fresh towels," Trufante answered and opened the door.

"Don't!" It was too late. Trufante turned, his arms filled with fresh towels. Mac thought for a second before jumping out of bed and pulling his pants on. "Hurry up. We've got to move."

"What up? They got good service, might as well take advantage of it," Trufante said and headed to the shower. "You used all the other ones. Got some umbrella drinks on the way too."

"The ship's security might be rent-a cops, but they're smart enough to know there's only one way off the boat, and we are still here. By now they are sure to have checked the roster of the cruisers who went ashore," he said. Mac reached down and picked up Trufante's clothes, tossed them to him, and finished dressing. "Hurry up. They could be here any second."

Mac waited with his ear to the door, listening for any sound in the hall while Trufante dressed. When the Cajun was ready, he turned the handle, eased the door open and peered into the corridor. Two uniformed men with radios lingered by the elevator. He closed the door and went to the desk where the brochure lay open, checked the deck plans confirming that deck four, where they had come aboard, was the only labelled exit point. He looked towards the window. There was no egress from the porthole, but he could see the open decks of the lifeboats below.

"Get on the phone and call something in on deck nine," he said and went back to the brochure. Trufante picked up the phone and cleared his throat. Mac gave him a hard look that said, *don't screw this up*, and went back to the brochure. He needed to find another way off the boat besides the excursion access. There was an unmarked opening on deck two that he guessed was for the baggage. Trufante was on the phone, playing the enraged tourist, yelling that someone was trying to break into his room. Mac went back to the door, cracked it open and watched the hallway, signaling Trufante to his side. Even though he was ready for it, the sound of the walkie-talkie startled him. One of the men put the radio to his ear and responded, then said something to the other and they headed towards them.

Mac's heart beat fast as he closed the door and waited. Of all the bad spots he had been in, being cornered was not a good place for him. A few seconds later, he re-opened the door, relieved the ruse had worked.

"We gotta go," he whispered and stepped into the hallway. Trufante followed and they walked past the elevator towards the sweeping stairway. The boat was crowded, the tourists returning from their shore activities, and he bumped into a crowd carrying bags with the name of the stores on Duval Street on their sides, more than several red-faced and stumbling. The kids were excited, talking about their snorkelling and para-sailing adventures.

They fought the tide of tourists going upstairs, passed deck four and descended to deck two. Mac had seen two unmarked access points on the plan and hoped one would lead off the ship. The hall was narrow and he tried to be patient, dodging more tourists entering and exiting their cabins. He reached the center of the deck and found the gap he was looking for, a sealed hatch door with a sign that an alarm would sound if it was opened. Raising an alarm would draw immediate attention and with that choice removed, he moved back through the deck, checking to make sure Trufante was still behind him, and climbed the stairs back to deck four. The horn blast startled him and he realized they were out of time. Not sure if it was just a warning or the signal to depart, he ran past the excursion desk, bumping into a woman in a cruise uniform.

"I left something on the launch! My kid is screaming," he pleaded. "Please let me have a look."

"Sir, the launch is gone."

Mac ignored her and pushed past to the opening where they had boarded earlier. There were several men working to close the gate and prepare the ship for departure. He saw the bow lines being released and felt the deck move underneath him as the engines increased RPMs. He knew he had to make his move now. He pushed past one of the men and jumped the gap to the pier.

"Go!" he called to Trufante.

***

Davies stepped out of the car, handed the driver his fare, plus another twenty to wait, and walked into the lobby of the hospital. He struggled to put his game face on as he approached a man in a sheriff's uniform flirting with the nurses behind the admissions desk.

"Sheriff DeLong?" he asked and waited for the man to turn his attention away from the blonde he was talking to. The man didn't respond. He called the name again.

This time he turned. "You Davies?" he asked. "Good to see you." He looked around the lobby. "Where's the Marshall?"

Davies had an answer ready, knowing the question was going to come. "They released me on my own recognizance," he answered. "Said I was to turn myself in to you when I got here."

"Hmm," the man murmured and put his hands on his hips. "Well, welcome to Marathon. You want to go up and see the girl?"

Davies bowed his head as if he was in mourning. "Yes, please. And I'd like to talk to the doctors as soon as it can be arranged."

The sheriff turned to the nurse. "Sweetheart, can you let them know we're heading up, and see if you can round up the doctor."

Davies followed him towards a bank of elevators. The doors opened and they waited while an attendant pushed an empty wheelchair into the lobby. The sheriff put his hand on the door and allowed Davies to enter first, then released it and they were alone in the cab.

The sheriff hesitated before pushing a button. "Seems you're the one to make the decision here," he said. "Girl's not in good shape, you know, and likely facing charges. They say her boyfriend, that Travis fellow, is dead."

Davies caught his drift and realized their goals were aligned. "I've been in this position before, and regrettable as it was, I can make hard decisions." He hoped the sheriff caught his drift.

"Yeah, hard as all hell, but sometimes it's for the best," the sheriff responded and pushed the button for Mel's floor.

The elevator rose and they were silent, both understanding they had the support of the other. Davies breathed in and out, regulating his breath like he used to do before entering a courtroom. The doors opened and he was ready. The two men walked past the nurses' station and several glass-fronted rooms before the sheriff stopped in front of one.

"She's in here. You want to go in, you can, but she hasn't regained consciousness."

"I'd like a minute, if I can," Davies answered and entered the room. Mel lay propped up in the bed, almost unrecognizable behind the bruises. Her head had been shaved to treat the numerous cuts on her scalp. A breathing tube was inserted in her mouth and a suction tube taped to her nose. He looked over at the monitor, beeping quietly in the background, and watched the graph showing her heart rate and vital signs. How easy it would be to just trip over the plug and end this, he thought, but he was close enough to doing it legally. One more look at his old apprentice, turned nemesis, and he left the room, not surprised there were no flowers.

"Darn shame," he told the sheriff. "Girl's got no kin and you say that boyfriend of hers is dead?"

He listened patiently as the sheriff recapped what he knew of the wreck and search. "Shut down the search last night."

Davies pursed his lips and shook his head. "Any chance of talking to the doctor? I hate to see her suffer like this."

"I told them you were coming, but they said you needed to talk to the ethics committee. Something about procedure. The best I could do was to get a meeting at eight tomorrow morning."

Davies shook his head again and looked through the glass window, then looked away as if he couldn't bear the pain of watching her suffer. What he was really thinking was how this was slowing down his personal timeline. The longer he stayed in the country the better the chance someone would start asking questions as to why he was living large in Marathon.

* * *
***

Another blast from the horn covered the screams from the staff on the cruise ship. Mac landed on the pier and rolled forward. Trufante landed on his feet next to him. A second blast sounded and he looked back to see the gate closed. They ran across the large landing area, but found it funneled into a narrow sidewalk with a closed security gate at the end. Two guards were gathering their belongings, about to leave, their shifts finished after verifying all the cruisers had come back. He looked around for another exit. The ground vibrated below them as the cruise ship moved away from the pier. The water was the only way off the pier and he was about to jump when he saw the jet skis tied up on the other side by a Fury Watersports sign. He glanced over the rail and saw a wooden dock below the concrete pier. The guards at the gate were talking to each other, not paying attention, their shifts over. Before they were noticed, he scaled the low fence and jumped the gap, landing feet first on the dock. He almost lost his balance when the floating structure rocked with his impact. He recovered and he fell to his knees watching Trufante land like a cat next to him.

They appeared to have been unobserved. The attention of anyone nearby was focused on the departure of the cruise ship. He started walking down the dock, trying to look casual, but his heart beat hard inside his chest. Just as he reached the concrete sidewalk leading to Front Street, the phone in his pocket rang.

He stopped under a palm tree and looked around to see if anyone had any interest in them. He withdrew the phone and opened the cover.

"Yes," he answered and listened to the voice on the other end. "I know the place." He listened for a minute. "I need more time," he stuttered in response and ended the call. He looked around to see if anyone was watching them and started walking towards the cover of the street. The man had asked for them to meet at a gas station on Stock Island. He fished around in his pocket and had a moment of panic before he realized Trufante had driven the car last.

"You still got the car keys?" he asked.

Trufante stuck his hand in his pocket and nodded. Mac picked up the pace as they followed Front Street and turned right onto Eaton. They had to push through the throngs of tourists milling around Duval, but the crowd thinned and they were able to pick up their pace. Mac guessed a half hour had elapsed when Eaton turned into Palm and they could see the marina. They reached Annie's car a few minutes later and he nodded for Trufante to drive. He looked at the clock on the dashboard as Trufante pulled into traffic. They were almost ten minutes late already and all he could see were brake lights ahead of him.

TWELVE

Mac paced back and forth, unsure if they had blown it by being late or the other man had yet to arrive. He was about to go to the hobos camped in the back corner of the lot when he remembered the phone in his pocket, took it out and hit the button to pull up the call history. The only entry on the screen showed a restricted number. He closed the cover and started pacing again. The two hobos must have sensed his mood, started gathering their gear and quickly moved out. Trufante sat on the curb by the back door eating a candy bar he had bought, a sixteen ounce can in a brown paper bag besides him. Mac had no appetite. He wanted this meeting over and was worried about Mel. The last words from the CIA man still echoed in his head, but to help Mel, or even see her, he had no choice but to follow his orders and clear his name.

A rental car pulled in and parked in a back corner by the air and water station. He heard his name called and turned to the car.

Norm leaned on the trunk. "Travis," he called again.

Mac walked toward him, glancing behind to make sure Trufante had remained where he was. He had decided it would be better to meet alone and if things went badly, Trufante would be far enough away to get help. What kind of help, or how badly things could go wrong, he didn't know.

The man crossed his arms. "Glad you had the sense to meet me," he said.

Mac crossed his arms in the same position and waited.

"Like I said, you need me. I am in the unique position to make your problems go away. I can set this all up to look like you were working for me on a CIA sting all along, and it all disappears. You can have your sorry old life back."

"Go on," Mac said.

"The baseball player is in the Krome Processing Center. I'm sure he has declared his intention to seek political asylum, either in his own words or the ones the authorities prepped him with. Either way, his government wants him back."

"What's that got to do with me? Put him on a plane and send him back," Mac said.

"If it was only so easy." He shook his head back and forth as if looking for sympathy. "The Cuban government is divided. Castro is frustrated that the United States is just giving enough in the new trade agreement to stop him from dealing with China. But, as beneficial as trade and China's money would be, they are scared of them as a partner. Like the Russians, they could pull out at any time, leaving them where they were when the USSR collapsed and stopped aid in the late '80's. At least with the US they know what they are going to get. Once trade opens, it will never close. The greedy corporations are already gearing up."

Travis was confused. International politics held little interest for him, but if he only needed to get Armando back to Cuba and he was done, he didn't really care. "What assurance do I have that you will follow through with this?"

Norm paused. "My word."

Mac laughed. "That's not going to do it and you know it."

"An act of good faith then?"

Mac knew he was being manipulated, but also knew he had no other options. "I'm listening."

"I'll get you into the hospital to see her." He stopped. "Tonight."

Mac tried not to show his excitement. "You do that, get my boat released, and you have a deal. There are a couple of things we need." He started to put a list together in his head. "The car is not ours." He pointed to the yellow jeep. "We'll need something less conspicuous for transportation, and some cash."

"Get Armando out of Krome and I'll see what I can do about the boat," Norm said. "The rest of it will be waiting in Marathon." He looked at his watch. "Ten o'clock at your friend's apartment." He looked over to Trufante.

Mac thought before answering. He reconciled both sides and came to the conclusion that until he actually tried to get Armando back into Cuba, there was no harm in taking the next step - and he would get to see Mel.

"I'm in. But no boat, no Cuba."

***

Norm waited in the air-conditioning of the rental car outside the small house. It was almost eight pm, but the tropical sun still baked the island. Thunderheads had been building over the day; the relief they contained remained within. He had tried the door. No one answered. He was getting impatient. You weren't going to turn a stripper into a clandestine agent overnight, but at least she should be punctual for a paying gig, even though it wasn't what she was expecting. Over the years he had recruited dancers, bartenders, waitresses and cab-drivers to do his bidding. They were usually grateful for the cash and were, more often than not, willing to walk the line at the edge of the law. It had been loud in the bar and he hoped he had heard her accent correctly. Russian and Eastern Europeans placed a different value on life than many Americans and were willing to do things: things he needed done. They were here for a better life and knew that working in clubs was a step on the road to the American Dream, not the end of the road, like their white trash American counterparts. She was likely in the country illegally and with his promise of a green card for her help, he expected she would buy into his plan. For what he considered a small fee, he wanted her to keep an eye on Travis for him - no matter what it took. If she had the skills, he thought, this would be no problem. He checked his watch again.

Impatient, he went back to the house, stopping at a piece-of-crap Honda in the carport. He instinctively placed his hand on the hood to see how long it had been there. The hood was warm, almost hot, even sitting in the shade of the overhang. He walked around it, noticing the owner would have been better served to put the money spent on wide wheels, tinted windows and pin-striping into something else. A quick look at the house and he headed back to the rental car on the street, becoming more aware of his surroundings, expecting something was wrong. He opened the door and paused when a cab pulled up and the girl got out. He took one look and smiled. She would be worth some risk.

He closed the door, followed her into the house and reached behind his back for the grip of the nine-millimeter gun. Slowly he drew it and before she turned around he had it levelled at her head. She started to scream, but a man emerged from the kitchen with a shotgun. His suspicion had been accurate; she had set him up. He grabbed her around the neck and held the gun at her head.

"You need to leave," he said. The man looked like he was going to say something, but Norm pressed the gun into the girl's temple. "We understand each other?"

The shotgun hit the floor and the man went for the door.

"Wait." Norm released the girl and pulled a hundred dollar bill from his pocket. "You never saw me."

The man nodded, took the bill and went out. Norm heard the engine start and the tires squeal when the transmission was jammed in reverse. Through the window, he watched the car back into the street and jerk forward. A hundred yards down the street, he heard the boom of the radio. Shaking his head and wondering about the judgement of the girl for bringing someone to their rendezvous, he went to the door and turned the lock.

"He was not supposed to be here," she said, confirming the Russian accent. "I'm going to change."

"Before you go, can I ask you a question?" He dangled the carrot and she nodded. "What would you do for a green card?"

She winked and left the room.

He stood waiting in the living room of the 1940's era house, just like a hundred others originally built for the Navy when the base here was more active. The original hardwood floor needed refinishing, the walls needed paint and the decade-old air-conditioner, rattling and coughing in the window, was struggling to take the humidity out of the air. He looked around, knowing he should leave, but unable to move. Slowly the adrenaline started to fade and he relaxed. He needed a break and he suspected the man wouldn't be back until he spent the cash. He went to the kitchen and sat on one of the barstools.

She emerged and approached him, wearing a robe which swung casually open as if she had forgotten to tie it. He had intended to talk business first, but in this case, the goods were too tempting. He would talk to her later.

He was following her to the bedroom when he felt something slam into his head.

THIRTEEN

Alicia Phon sat in the agency's Taurus, with the air-conditioning running. She was nervous and tapped the wheel, frantic that her antiperspirant was not working. She looked down at the small stains on her silk blouse thinking she might need to rethink her field attire. The call had come as a surprise and there was no way she was going to turn down her first opportunity for field work, but he had given her no time to change. Miami, where she was based, was humid, but this was on another level; everything here was either wet or at least damp. Used to a sterile computer room, she lived in air-conditioning: her apartment, her office, her car; even the gym was climate-controlled. Somehow, after the last five years behind a computer, she had been given a shot. She was scared, but she was also determined, a trait she had gotten from her Dragon Mom mother. This is what she had joined the CIA for.

A yellow jeep pulled into the lot and she tried to pull herself together. She put on her jacket, breathed deeply, left the air-conditioning and walked across the gravel, carefully placing each step of her high heels as she crossed the parking lot. She kept her head high, as she had been taught in finishing school, although she couldn't have felt more out of place.

***

The trail of empty bottles and remnants of the party at Trufante's apartment extended almost to US 1, growing denser as they pulled into the parking area. Without the host and his bankroll, the party had died, but the fallout was evident. Mac pulled into a parking space, carefully avoiding a beer bottle perched on the curb. They climbed out and navigated the path to Trufante's door.

"Mac Travis?" a voice called.

He looked back and saw a thirty-something-year-old woman, more like a girl, dressed in a business suit, come towards him. If this was Norm's idea of help, he was in trouble.

"Yeah," he growled.

"My name is Alicia Phon. I am assigned to help you." Her voice cracked.

"Chi-fon," Trufante repeated with his thick Cajun accent as he came towards them, towering over the diminutive girl.

There was no point in discussing this in the parking lot and he decided it was better to get away from prying eyes and ears. "Hey. Sure. Let's go inside."

Trufante's door was ajar. Mac pushed it open, calling inside to see if anyone was there before entering. He turned on the light and looked around at the trashed apartment, moved over to the kitchen table and pushed its contents onto the floor.

"Nice friends you got," he said to Trufante, who was looking in the refrigerator and turned back to him empty-handed. Mac pulled out the phone and checked the time, anxious to get out of there. It was 9:45, only fifteen minutes to wait. "Might as well take Annie's car back. I'll pick you up after I see Mel." He noticed the hurt look on Trufante's face. "I'm thinking we'll stay here for now and head upstate in the morning. Nothing to be done up there tonight," he said.

Trufante's mood rebounded, probably after he realized he had all night to party. He took the keys from Mac and left the room, the thousand-dollar smile on his face. Mac sat at the table and waited while the girl carefully cleared a space on the couch and sat down. They sat in silence, looking each other over, neither knowing where to start.

"I can get you into the hospital," she said finally. "I'm very good with a computer too."

"Yeah, what's the plan?" Mac answered, wanting no part in small talk.

"We can work that out later. Let's get you in to see your girlfriend."

He started towards the door. "OK. One step at a time."

She reached into her bag and handed him some scrubs.

Mac took them from her. At least there was some level of planning going on here. "I'm gonna clean up. Make yourself at home," he told the girl and went for the bathroom.

He finished a quick shower, toweled off, and winced as he picked up Trufante's razor to shave. A look in the mirror at his week-old growth changed his mind. It itched like crazy, but it changed his appearance enough that he decided to leave it. He put on the scrubs and went back into the living room where the girl was dumping bottles and cans into a large trash bag.

"You don't have to do that," he said, watching her continue. "Why don't we get a bite to eat and talk about your plan. Does the CIA have an expense account?" he asked, fingering the loose change in his pocket.

"OK," she said, grabbed her messenger bag and headed for the door.

***

Davies walked into the room with a coffee cup in one hand and his briefcase in the other, feeling just like old times. He was late after failing to find a Starbucks, having to settle for a local shop for his mocha latte. The group of doctors looked at him, impatient for his decision.

"Mr. Davies," the head doctor started, "do you have questions for us?"

Davies took a sip of his drink, enjoying the flavor as he looked at the tired doctors sitting behind the table, drinking coffee from styrofoam cups. He opened his briefcase and removed a legal pad. "I have talked to several of her doctors already. If you can confirm the prognosis, I believe we can make a decision.

"Go ahead," the doctor said.

"You have not declared her brain dead. She is in a coma and breathing with a ventilator. Aren't those the requirements?" he asked.

The doctor paused, as if it was painful to educate the man. "The protocol we use is based on the AAN's 2010 guidelines. Of the three tests involved, she can only be confirmed with one, and I am a little uneasy declaring that. Ms. Woodson has only been with us for three days. None of her symptoms meet the permanent status called for. Although she needs the help of the ventilator, she is breathing on her own. It is erratic and shallow, but cannot be disregarded. The only conclusive damage we can determine is that her reflexes are not working, but that could be temporary paralysis."

Davies started to say something, but the doctor cut him off, thinking he was anticipating the question. "Will she ever wake up and be able to function? I don't know."

These were not the answers he was hoping for, but he was prepared. He withdrew a document from his briefcase and handed it to the doctor next to him, who scanned it and passed it along. "You can see that this is her living will and she is clear that her life is to be terminated if her quality of life is reduced to the point it is." He lowered his head before continuing, "I don't have a choice but to concede to her wishes."

The doctors exchanged glances. "Mr. Davies, I appreciate your concern, but I have to object. Three days is not long enough to make a final diagnosis. I recommend we wait at least another forty-eight hours before making a life or death decision."

Davies hid behind his coffee, sipping while he thought. Two more days was not in his timeline. There were too many loose ends in his escape plan that could unravel in that time. He didn't expect the sheriff to be a problem, but anything could happen and the sooner he was out of the country, the better. The doctor's timeline was not acceptable.

"It is my duty to enforce her wishes. I know a specialist in brain injuries in Miami. Would anyone object to a consultation from him?" Davies knew a doctor who owed him a favor. The group nodded their heads in agreement; thankful the decision would be taken from their hands.

"We would welcome another opinion," the doctor responded.

One by one the doctors and administrators left the room. He was left alone with his premium coffee amongst the discarded styrofoam cups. He gathered the cups in a circle, took the last swig from his and placed it on top of theirs.

***

Mac and Alicia huddled around her tablet as rain beat down on the roof of the Taurus. He looked up to make sure no one was watching them, but the windows were fogged.

"That's her room," Alicia pointed at the tablet. "Fourth floor: sixth door on the left after the nurses' station."

Mac stared at the screen showing a floor plan of the hospital. "OK," he said and pulled a ball cap over his face. He left the car and ran towards the entrance to the hospital, pausing to glance back at the car. He wasn't sure how much to trust this woman. Although she was competent with a computer, she also worked for Norm. The girl was nervous and had made several comments that this was the first field mission she had been on and from the look of her suit and heels, he wondered if she could handle things when they went bad. He knew they inevitably would – they always did. Her computer-generated plans would fall apart at some point. It was one thing to push some buttons sitting in an air-conditioned office drinking lattes, but in the real world things went wrong - often badly.

He ran through the storm to the portico and waited under cover of the hospital entrance. Thunder crashed and the lights flickered. A second later they went back on, and as if on cue, another blast hit and the building went dark. The storm had been a blessing, allowing them the diversion Mac would need to get inside unrecognized. Alicia had control of the complex's power and had assured him that it was safe. The hospital had a huge bank of backup generators and emergency lighting to ensure life support and essential systems would not be affected by the frequent storms.

Generators kicked on and the building lit to half-power. This was the signal. He pulled the bill of the hat over his face and went inside. The stairwell to the right of the elevators was crowded and he squeezed his way past several people in scrubs and started up the stairs. He pulled the phone from his pocket when he reached the fourth floor and checked the time; fifteen minutes until she turned the power on. Slowly he opened the door and entered the hallway. The nurses' station was bustling with activity. He walked by and started counting doors.

The room was open and he entered a small waiting area with another door and a large window directly in front of him. He set his hand on the handle, but she had warned him that if he opened the door it would send a signal to the nurses' station. Frustrated, he released the lever and walked over to the window. Mel lay propped up in bed, almost unrecognizable, her hair shaved and tubes running through and around her, the green light cast by the bank of monitors doing nothing to make her look alive. He stared at her, soothed slightly by the rhythmic beeping of her heart. There was nothing else he could do, but it was good to know she was alive.

He watched through the glass and whispered that he loved her. One more look and he left the room and went towards the stairs where he waited by the door as several doctors and nurses came out before entering the stairwell. He took the steps two at a time, not wanting to be caught in the building when the lights came back on. He flew around the landing to the second floor and ran head on into a man dressed in a lab coat, also moving too fast, the force of the impact landing both men on the floor. Mac got up first and extended his hand to help the other man to his feet when he noticed the pill bottles that had spilled from the deep pockets of the coat. The man met his glance and he froze.

"Larry?"

"Travis. Is that you?" The man calmly collected the bottles and stood up. "You're supposed to be dead," He tried to push past Mac.

Mac grabbed him by the shoulder and spun him around. "Maybe we should go outside and have a little chat. Looks like you haven't changed." He picked up one of the bottles and read the label for the powerful painkiller.

The man looked away, eyes darting to the people passing on the stairs. "Might be able to help you out if this stays between us," he said, and started down the stairs.

They walked outside and around the building, staying under the eaves to avoid the rain. By the garbage enclosure, Mac pushed him against the wall. "My patience is short for you," he said, and waited for the man to reply. Back when they were working together, Mac and Wood had burned through help at a rapid pace. They were either too demanding or the help was lax, the latter more often the case in the transient capital of the world, and Larry had been one of the slackers they had fired.

"What? I feel bad about Wood's daughter," he said.

Mac ignored him, knowing there were no feelings. "You stealing drugs." It was a statement. "What's going to stop me from turning you in?"

The man looked at him as if he was about to play a royal flush, "Like I said. I got something you might want to hear."

Mac glared at him, biting back the feeling that he wanted to hit him.

"Big shot lawyer from Virginia or someplace is here to make the decisions about her. Seems they all think that you're dead. There's talk of bringing a specialist from Miami to see if she is brain dead or not. The clocks tickin', buddy."

Mac pushed him aside and ran for the car.

FOURTEEN

Mac woke the next morning with a beer bottle poking him in the side. It would have been a sleepless night wherever he had found himself, the image of Mel refusing to leave him. Alicia had dropped him off after the visit with Mel at the hospital and he had found the house empty. He thought about taking Trufante's bed, but he wasn't sure what might live there, so he crashed on the couch.

Not sure if the Cajun was home, he went towards the bedroom and peeked in the open door. A body moved in the bed and he walked away. The kitchen was a disaster area: the counters covered with old food and empty beer bottles. The stale stench overpowered him and forced him to abort his search for coffee. What little clean-up Alicia had started last night was invisible.

He reached into his pocket and pulled out the phone to check the time. There were still two hours before Alicia was due back to pick him up for the trip to Krome and he knew he couldn't just sit and wait. The palm fronds, visible through the half-closed blinds, swayed softly in the breeze and he guessed the inshore waters would be calm. A great morning to be out on the flats fishing with the breeze disturbing the water just enough to disguise a fisherman's movements, but he had no chance of that. He thought some exercise might help him think though, so he grabbed a pair of Trufante's running shoes, slipped them on and headed out the door. He stopped on the landing and went back in for the ball cap to hide his face.

He started at a walk until he reached the Heritage Trail running parallel to US1 and then increased the pace to an easy jog, heading west towards the Seven Mile Bridge. Not really a runner, he couldn't help restrain himself and increased his speed near his old street - old as in a week ago. He fought against himself, knowing it was stupid for too many reasons to list, but couldn't resist the urge to check on the damage to his house. After waiting for the light to change, he pulled the bill on the cap over his face, sprinted across the four-lane highway and slowed to a jog as he reached his street. Sweat poured off him and although it was uncomfortable, he was thankful the morning humidity, a side effect of last night's storm, was enough to keep his neighbors inside their air-conditioned houses.

The charred smell hit him before he reached the house and he stood back in shock. The roof was caved in and half of the second floor walls where the missile had hit were gone. A temporary chain link fence secured the boundaries of the property with yellow police tape ringing the house itself. He looked around to make sure no one was watching, slid between the intersection of the fence panels at the corner of the lot and went around back, staying close to the unstable structure. The roll-up door in back was caved in, but the main door was open and he entered the workshop.

Rain water dripped through cracks in the ceiling and he dodged the drips and he went for the workbench. Most of the tools and equipment were covered in soot and water, but remained where he had left them. He moved past the work area and went to the office. It was dark and his hand instinctively moved to the light switch, even though he knew the power was off. Back at the workbench, he dug around for a flashlight and froze. The sound of a car pulling into the driveway startled him and he wondered if one of his neighbors had seen and reported him.

He ran back to the office and turned on the flashlight. The walls and desk were smoke-stained and wet. A door slammed outside and he hurried, taking the computer console and yanking the cover from it. With the flashlight propped under his chin, he pulled the hard drive loose and shoved it into the pocket of his cargo pants. Another door slammed and he knew he had to move fast. The door to the safe was ajar, the way he remembered leaving it when he escaped only days ago. The contents were not where he remembered them though, and he expected the authorities had searched it, but he moved his hand up to the lid and felt for the thumb drive he had taped in place. Not surprised it was gone, he moved his hand to where the revolver had sat.

Two men were talking out front and he heard the unmistakable sound of a police radio. The revolver was gone as well, and he came up with only a handful of bullets. He tossed them on the floor and slid quietly out the door, turning off the flashlight as he moved towards the back of the workshop. The voices were still out front and he was about to run out the back door and seek cover when he saw the rack that held his stand up paddleboards. The two SUPs, one narrow and sleek for speed, the other wide and shorter for fishing, were still in the rack. A floor joist from the ceiling rested on the streamlined racing board, his first choice for an escape, the fragile board split where it had landed. The wider fishing board on the bottom of the rack looked serviceable.

Someone was coming around the house and he knew he was out of time. With the board clutched under on arm and a paddle in the other, he went for the door. A sideways glance confirmed the man had not reached the back. He made a beeline for the dock and jumped with the board glued to his belly and the paddle by his side. The board hit the water, landing perfectly underneath him and planed over the water. He quickly stood and started paddling. A voice yelled for him to stop, but there was no threat behind it and he thought he was far enough away there was a chance the officer thought he hadn't heard it. With long and deceivingly powerful strokes, so it appeared to an onlooker he was out for a leisurely paddle, he pulled the board forward over the water and left the cover of the canal leading to Boot Key Harbor.

The wind was in his face when he reached open water and he struggled to make headway, but with the police behind him, there was only one place to go and that was forward. He fought to make every stroke count as he made his way into the harbor, the tip of the board slamming each wave as he moved toward the gas docks along the north shore. He stepped forward on the board to sink the nose into the swells and gained a bit of speed. Grounding, although possible in the tidal area, was not a concern with the shallow draft board, and he paddled onto the flats by Hog Key. He was more worried the police had recognized him and called in backup than he was of getting stuck in the backwater. It would be hard, but he could walk out of the muck. He wasn't so sure he could walk away from the police. He paddled into the skinny water on the side of the channel, moving his weight even further forward to bring the fin almost out of the water, using sweeping strokes to steer without the aid of the rudder. Even with the fin only inches in the water, it brushed bottom several times, but the board only drew a few inches and he had to use the paddle to pole himself several times. He moved back on the board when muddy bottom finally turned to sand and gained some depth, then made his way around Knight Key and crossed under the first span of the Seven Mile Bridge.

The paddling was easier with the wind at his back and he stroked to deeper water after checking he wasn't being followed. The Fanny Keys blew by on his right and he started to enjoy the downwind paddle. He concentrated on the shoreline as the wind helped push him by the numerous canals and small lagoons along the coast, not sure which one led to Trufante's. The airport was the best landmark to find the narrow canal and as he passed between Rachel Key and the point of land projecting from the mainland, he could see the runway ahead.

The sound of a siren startled him. He almost lost his balance and fell from the board, and for the first time he was thankful he had taken the wider board. He looked towards the bay, saw a Zodiac police boat stopping a kayak and pulled harder, hoping the report was wrong and they were looking for a kayak, not a SUP. Two canals lay ahead and he went for the far one, glancing over his shoulder at the police boat and turned. The officers were finished with the kayaker and had spotted him. Mac froze for a second as the siren blared. He knew they wanted him.

The only thing he could do was to paddle harder. He doubled his stroke rate, putting everything he had into it, not caring that it looked like he was fleeing. The Zodiac entered the canal and the siren blared again, but he was in a shallow channel barely wide enough for the boat, with the refuge of the mangroves just ahead. He pushed forward, knowing the police boat would have to slow or risk fouling their propeller in the gnarly root system of the trees, and headed straight into a gap in the brush. The fin snagged a root and he was launched forward, saving himself from the water only by grabbing an overhead branch and swinging to what looked like dry land.

He chanced a look back at the police boat, idling by, both men searching the shoreline. Unreachable in the brush, he pulled the board towards him, stashed it by the trunk of a lignum vitae tree, and ran to an austere commercial building in a small clearing. After clearing the brush he made an all-out sprint towards it. He knew the police would be searching there any minute. He pulled the phone from his pocket, flipped it open and hit the button Alicia had programmed in for her cell phone.

She answered on the first ring, annoyed that he wasn't at Trufante's waiting for her. He pulled the phone from his ear and looked at the time. She was right; he was fifteen minutes late.

"Scold me later. Right now get me out of here," he said, "and you better take Trufante too. The police are after me and somehow he'll stumble into them if he's around. The boy's just got that kind of luck." He pulled the phone away and closed the cover in the middle of her sentence. The last thing he needed right now was a self-righteous rant from a desk agent; he needed her to concentrate on the task at hand.

The phone rang a minute later and he quickly flipped the lid to stop the sound, fumbling with the volume button. "Tell me where to go," he whispered, hoping his calmness permeated the line.

"You are just around the corner. Walk out to Aviation Boulevard and turn left at the first driveway. We will be waiting." She hung up.

Mac started walking, wondering at the same time how she knew where he was. He was impressed that after her initial rant, she had calmed down and handled the situation. He looked both ways, half-expecting a police car to appear when he crossed Aviation, and ran across the clearing to the building on the corner.

He stood there for what seemed like an eternity. Finally her car approached and he got in. "What happened?"

"Couldn't find my damn shoes," Trufante grumbled from the back, still buttoning up a grimy safari shirt.

Mac turned to tell him where his shoes were and noticed a police cruiser turn into the apartment complex. Alicia must have seen it in her rearview mirror. She turned onto the frontage road instead of the highway, slowly increasing speed as they sped past the lone runway. Several hangers and a field with a handful of aircraft appeared on the side. She turned to the general aviation building, cut through the parking lot and caught a green light for the turn onto US 1.

"Think we can eat before we gotta rescue Armando?" Trufante asked from the back.

Mac and Alicia looked at each other and laughed.

FIFTEEN

Bradley Davies paced back and forth outside the hospital, careful to avoid the puddles from last night's rain. He checked his watch and the entrance after each lap, wondering if it rained this much in Cuba. He had picked up a guidebook for the island that now held a prominent position in his briefcase. The financial opportunities there, now that the US had opened trade relations along with what he was sure would remain a no extradition policy, made the island alluring. Finding the nightlife in Marathon substandard - meaning unless you were into dive bars and beach bands, there was none - he had eaten a surprisingly good meal at the Barracuda Grill and gone back to his hotel room to read the book, cover to cover.

The history and architecture of the island surprised him. The constant notion that "tourists are king" only increased the appeal of the nation - and they had nightlife. Already a popular destination with European and Canadian tourists, the lifting of the transportation ban from the United States would truly make it a hotspot. Not one to trust the communist government with his assets he still planned on keeping what money he had left in the Cayman Islands.

A cab pulled into the lot, interrupting his thoughts. He went to the curb and waited.

An olive-skinned man exited the back seat and looked at Davies. "Pay the man, would you," he said and walked past him to the entrance.

Davies followed behind, moving quickly to open the door. "Thanks for coming down so quickly. I really appreciate it."

The man stopped at the threshold. "You know how you can show your appreciation. I have not gotten a confirmation from my bank yet."

"Just wanted to make sure everything was cool. I'll make the transfer while you examine her," Davies said and followed the man to the reception counter where he presented his credentials and received a visitor's pass from the smiling nurse. Her smile turned to a scowl when Davies glanced at her.

They rode the elevator to the fourth floor and were met at the nurses' station by a doctor who shook the man's hand, while not so discreetly ignoring the lawyer. They chatted briefly and he led the way to Mel's room. Davies waited in the small foyer as the two men went inside. He sat in one of the vinyl upholstered chairs and started working through the unfamiliar screen of the smart phone. Technology had changed since his incarceration, but finally he fumbled through the screens and initiated the transfer. He expected no trouble from the local doctor, who was probably grateful for the specialist to take responsibility for the case. A few minutes later the men exited the room, shook hands, and the doctor left.

"Everything good?" Davies asked the man.

"Have to review the tests and do a little dog and pony show for the locals, but if you handle your end, I'll take care of mine," he said and walked out of the room. "I'll contact you later."

Davies watched him talking to the nurse behind the desk. They shared a laugh and he was jealous of the look she gave him. Should have been a doctor, he thought as he waited for the elevator, but then decided it would have been too much work.

***

Norm opened one eye and then the other, realizing the buzzing he felt in his chest was the satellite phone. He rolled over, fighting the throbbing in his head, and reached for it. Through bloodshot, half-closed eyes, he tried to make out the number, but it didn't register.

"Hello," he said, holding the phone with one hand while he rubbed the large knot on his head with the other. Dried blood was visible on his hand when he looked at it.

"*Mi amigo.*"

The voice on the other end startled him awake. He struggled to his knees and then his feet, checked the house, confirming he was alone. His decision to find a little diversion last night after the plan was set in motion had turned out badly. One of the many problems he had faced after being forced into an administrative job was that he had no control once the mission started. Used to running his own operations, this had set him on edge, causing him to sit in his office late into the night, guessing and wondering if things were unfolding as planned. Of course they never did due to a principle called friction he remembered from studying military history, made famous by a Prussian General named Clausewitz. The most thorough and detailed plans always changed when the opposition reacted – always. Without the ability to direct the operations, he had taken to drinking and whoring on those nights, the only way he could ease his mind.

"Why are you calling me?" he asked in Spanish.

"I have not heard from you: such a simple operation for so experienced a man." The voice paused, losing patience. "Where is my grandson? You have less than forty-eight hours."

Norm tried to clear his head and looked over at the windows, realizing it was morning. He calculated the time. "That's Saturday morning."

"Yes. The initial run of the ferry," the man said. "And you need to have my grandson on it."

"Don't hit me with veiled threats," he countered.

"It is not a veiled threat. It is a direct threat. You know that ferry service harms China."

Norm needed to stall and think this through. "Everything is in motion," he said and disconnected the call.

The house would not be empty for long. He expected the couple home any time after whatever party they had found exhausted his money. He reached in his pockets and found them empty, both his keys and wallet gone. The only reason the satellite phone was not taken was the special holster he used under his shirt. He left the house, saw the rental car missing and started walking, his anger building. This ferry was going to be a security nightmare, the perfect showcase for both sides to express anger pent up over five decades.

The timeline started clicking in his head as he reached Atlantic Boulevard, where he stood and watched the waves break against the beach. Travis should be on his way back from Krome in a few hours. He needed to get him to Key West quickly. A seaplane buzzed over his head and he thought that might be the answer.

His plan had encountered friction already, only hours after starting. He had planned to insert the men into Cuba by boat and then have them swim in with the aid of a dive scooter, his typical method for inserting operatives, but Choy's demand of having Armando on the ferry changed everything. What if he wasn't aboard? The general could be blowing smoke, but the risks in ignoring his threats were large. He needed to reach Alicia.

On a nearby bench he sat, pulled out his phone, scrolled through his contacts and pressed send. The phone rang and went to voicemail, Alicia's nervous voice saying she wasn't available. He wasn't really worried; the girl was so reliable and eager. There probably wasn't service out by Krome.

***

The trio headed north on US1 in silence. Alicia had turned over the wheel to Trufante and was pecking at her phone while Mac tried to relax after his morning adrenaline rush.

"How 'bout some food?" Trufante asked again.

"Find a place with WIFI," Alicia said, not lifting her head. "It's still early. Visitors' hours aren't until nine and I'd rather wait till eleven when it is more crowded and the guards start to take their lunch breaks."

They were almost to Key Largo when Trufante made a sharp turn into the parking lot of an upscale resort. "Only thing I've seen," he said and pulled into a parking space.

"Long as you're buying," Mac said, hoping there was still some money left from the sale of the boat.

They walked into the lobby, turned into the restaurant and waited to be seated. A hostess came over and eyed them suspiciously, but Alicia said something to soothe her and they were seated in a booth by the kitchen.

Mac glanced at the menu, watching Alicia out of the corner of his eye as she pulled a tablet from her messenger bag and started typing. The waitress came over with coffee, took their order and they were left alone.

"You been doing this CIA thing for a while?" Mac asked.

"I graduated Stanford in '08. Kicked around Silicon Valley for a while, but got tired of working on code; finding more often than not you do all the crazy hours and deadlines, and it's obsolete or somebody beat you to it before you're even finished. My brother had some friends that worked for the NSA and they hooked me up." She sipped her tea.

Mac had no doubt about her technical ability, but she didn't look like a field agent. "How much time in the field?" he asked. If she was guiding this mission, he hoped she had some experience.

She looked down. "This is my first time," she said shyly. "But it's a slam dunk security breach deal. I've done a bunch of these from the office."

The food arrived and he was able to end the conversation without hurting her. Maybe she was right and this was a computer game, and the last thing he wanted to do was to make it appear he doubted her abilities. He needed her focused. They finished the meal in silence and she went back to pecking at the screen after the table was cleared.

"So you have this all planned out?" he asked.

"To the minute; I drop you off and drive Tru to the airboat rental. You signal me with a text from this cell phone right before they let you in." She handed him another burner. "They're going to take the phone, but it's untraceable. As soon as I get the text, I initiate a sequence of alarms that should provide the diversion you need to get out. She reached in her pocket and handed him a small black key. "This is carbon fiber. The metal detectors won't pick it up. As soon as the guard leaves to answer the alarm, you open the restraints."

He took the key and slid it into his pocket, surprised by how light it was.

"It's delicate though. You might only get one shot at the locks. If you force it, it may break."

Great, Mac thought, give a breakable key to the guy that could break something by looking at it. "You better hold this one then," he said. "Your boss wouldn't want them to get a hold of it."

She frowned, took Norm's burner phone and held it delicately in her hands.

"And you'll be with numb-nuts here, so he knows what to do?" Mac quipped.

"I'm sitting right here," Trufante whined.

Mac ignored him and looked at her.

"No, he can rent the boat and meet you. There is no need for me," she said and ran her hands down the front of her expensive shirt.

The self conscious gesture was not lost on Mac. She was plainly out of her element and maybe it was best if she wasn't along if things got rough.

Trufante was bound to do something boneheaded along the way, but he was used to him and knew what to expect. She would be a total wildcard.

Her phone beeped and she looked down at the screen. "I have to take this. I'll meet you outside."

She got up and left. Mac looked over at Trufante, "Well, you might as well pay the bill. Looks like it's just me and you."

"Old times," Trufante said.

***

"It is under control," she said into the phone after walking outside and making sure no one was near. "We're in Key Largo. I just briefed them and we are headed to Krome now."

"You understand your mission?" he asked.

"Yes. Drop them off, stay on site until they are clear, and head back to the office." She repeated her orders.

"Good. And this is between us," he said.

She wondered why he was being secretive and turned the burner phone in her hands. They'd had several interactions before, when he needed her expertise or analysis, but it was always behind the walls of the office in Miami. She had asked to be assigned to the field several times, but was told she was too valuable where she was. The urge never left her, but even if she was destined to remain behind a desk, Miami was an upgrade from Silicon Valley, and the work was challenging.

"OK," she said, not wanting to give him an excuse to change his mind. "Whatever you say; I will initiate the alarms and monitor from my house."

Norm had taken her out of her comfort zone pretty quickly when he told her it would be better to work from home. She knew field operatives often did mundane tasks outside of the office, but with all the resources available there, surely it would be better. She started to feel self-conscious when she noticed her antiperspirant was failing again. Not sure if it was the stress or humidity, she thought maybe going home was a good idea.

"And one more thing." He paused. "Wipe it clean. This never happened."

The alarms were starting to go off in her head. The congressional inquiries concerning CIA covert activity over the last few years had initiated new protocols for archiving data and transparency. Working

83

from home and his request to erase all the data were not in the manual. But in the end, her desire to succeed in the field overrode her wariness.

"What about the promises you made to Travis?" she asked.

"Travis is dead: one way or another."

Everything she expected had gone haywire and she fought to keep her composure. She knew one of the first rules of tradecraft was to not get emotionally involved with your operatives, but she felt a strange kinship with the two men. There was no way not to feel for Mac, fighting to keep his girlfriend alive, but she knew enough to hold back. There was silence on the line and she looked at the screen. The call had been disconnected.

Mac and Trufante walked out the door and she wondered how they could be so easygoing right before they faced the unknown. She met them at the car, keeping her arms tight to her sides so they couldn't see the growing wet spots under them.

They sat in the car staring at her and it took her a minute to finally realize they were waiting for her to tell them what to do. A pit formed in her stomach and she tried to quell her uncertainty, about both the mission and her boss, in order to guide the escape. Her only consolation was that if the plan went totally off the rails, she had enough access to remove her involvement of the matter and make the whole thing go away. Norm had virtually given permission to erase everything.

"Let's go," she said weakly and swallowed hard, hoping they hadn't noticed.

Trufante pulled out of the lot and turned north on US 1. She pulled the tablet from her bag and immersed herself in the data flowing across the screen. Out of the corner of her eye, she saw Mac reach into his pocket and she flinched when she saw the glint of metal.

"You know how to get the files off this?" He handed her a hard drive.

She relaxed and took it from him, turning it in her hands and straining to read the embossed numbers. "Yes."

"I'd appreciate it if you could hold onto this and see what you can do."

She looked at the drive and was about to hand it back and tell him there were businesses that could do that, but saw the pleading look in his eyes and nodded.

"Thanks. It's personal stuff, not national security like you're used to." He leaned forward as if he had something else to say.

"What is it?" she asked.

"Can you use that thing to keep an eye on Mel?"

She knew it wasn't unusual for agents about to go into harm's way to ask their handlers for favors. "Sure," she said, but knew if she agreed that she was taking another step on the emotional ladder she had been warned against.

SIXTEEN

Mac hit the send button on the text he had already typed just before the guard took the phone and asked him to empty his pockets. Relieved he had given the hard drive to Alicia, he handed over the pocket knife and loose change, trusting her that the small carbon fiber key would not be detected. After a stroll through the metal detector, he followed the guard down a narrow hall with doors on each side. He tried to look through the small windows, but the view was obstructed by the wire mesh embedded inside the glass.

The man stopped in front of a door with the number fourteen on a small metal sign, looked through the safety glass and inserted a key into the lock. He pushed the door open and waited for Mac to enter.

"Fifteen minutes. If you need out sooner, hit the button by the door," the man said and turned to leave.

"I heard with a minimum security detainee, that we are allowed to go into the yard." Mac used the words Alicia had made him memorize. She had stressed the importance of saying detainee instead of prisoner.

The guard glared at him and turned toward the door. "I'll see if I can get you a pass. Wouldn't mind some fresh air myself."

Mac turned tentatively, no idea how Armando would react. "I'm glad to see you, my friend." He spoke in halting Spanish, again using the words Alicia had told him.

The Cuban sat in the metal chair, wrists and ankles shackled together and attached to bolts protruding from the floor. "*Mi amigo*, Mac," the man started. "I too am glad to see you." There were at least three cameras, Mac thought while surreptitiously scanning the room, each with a different angle of the chair Armando occupied. He was out of Spanish and nervously waited for the guard to return.

He could tell Armando was nervous as well. "*Vamanos*," he whispered and the man nodded.

The door opened and the guard entered. "We're good. You can have the yard for half an hour. I'll be watching, so no crap," he said and held the door. Mac exited and waited in the hall for the guard. Suddenly a buzzer went off in the room next door and he stood back as the guard rushed from the room joining several other men responding to the alarm. That was the first sign that Alicia had triggered the alarm and he started the countdown in his head to the next diversion.

More alarms sounded. Uniformed guards streamed into the hallway to answer the calls, confused by the red lights flashing everywhere. Carefully he eased the door closed so the latch didn't engage, and went to Armando. With the carbon-fiber key shaking in his fingers, he released the Cuban's ankles and they crossed to the door; his hands would have to wait. They had only seconds to get out of the building.

***

"That's the alarm," Alicia said. She stared at her tablet. She was regretting the decision to let Trufante drive, alarmed every time the car bounced on and off the gravel shoulder. She had the tablet on her lap, one eye on the screen, the other on the road. They were on highway 41, the southern of the two routes across The Everglades. Canals ran on both sides of the road, draining water from the swamp, known as the river of grass that covered South Florida, to accommodate the ever-increasing population. Decade old cars were pulled to the side where the trees allowed access to the water, clusters of families fishing with cane poles after the bass, gar and catfish.

"It's another few miles on the left. Gator Jim's," she said and resumed her vigil, staring at the screen, thankful for the satellite connection after noticing the austere surroundings. A small timer in the upper right of the screen counted down the time since the first alarm had gone off and she monitored the camera feed she had hacked into, watching what was happening in the detention facility in real time. She opened a text window and started typing the next set of instructions.

"Whatcha got going on there, Chi-fon?" Trufante asked. He peered over her shoulder. The car slammed against the gravel embankment and he looked back towards the road before she had to say anything.

She ignored the name. "It's a matrix of the security grid from ICE's server. From this I can lead them out and see where the alarms are sounding. I'm getting ready to create a diversion as soon as I see the alarm from the exterior door go," she said, staring at the screen.

"That it?" Trufante asked.

A parking lot appeared out of the wilderness of sawgrass and scrub, the only sign of life they had seen since the fishermen several miles ago. The car pulled into the gravel lot and coasted to a stop alongside a tour bus.

"Go in and rent an airboat," she said. She typed something else on the screen. "They are outside now and I'm about to set all hell loose. You're going to have to hurry to make the rendezvous." With a swipe of her finger, the screen changed to a satellite view of the area. "Here we are." She pointed. "It's a straight shot to meet them. First building you're going to see over the embankment is where they'll be."

"You ain't goin' with?" Trufante asked, opened the door and slid his tall frame out of the car.

"I have to manage this," she said and waited while he walked towards the entrance. She looked back down at the screen. So far so good, she thought. She typed a line of code. Seconds later the top left of the screen lit up with red dots. The alarm must have worked. She picked up the chatter in the text box about men being dispatched to the high security area where she had set off the smoke detectors. She waited several minutes, fascinated by the havoc she had caused by pressing a few buttons, and typed in another snippet of code that would deactivate the electric fence on the other side. An orange icon appeared on the disabled section of fence, but in the big picture, with the red dots indicating a higher security breach on the other side of the compound, it would probably be ignored or given minimal support.

It was up to Mac and the Cuban now, and she hoped he had memorized the plan. There was nothing else she could do to help after drawing off the guards and shutting down the fence. She slid the tablet into her messenger bag and got out to stretch her legs before heading back to Miami. Just as she got out, Trufante burst through the front door in a panic.

"I got no ID. They ain't renting me no boat," he said.

"No ID? Everyone has ID!" She couldn't believe it.

"Shit, Ain't no one giving me a credit card and I got no use for a license." He moved to the side as she brushed past.

She went for the glass door and paused. There was no choice but to use her ID and credit card. It was not what she had planned, and she would have to act quickly to erase the transaction from the credit card company's files, but the entire plan and her future hinged on getting the Cuban out of Krome, and this was their only chance.

"Here," she thrust her ID across the counter at the clerk. He took the driver's license and stood there in his straw cowboy hat comparing the picture to her face. Apparently Trufante had done little to engage the man's trust. "We are in kind of a rush," she said.

"I got the paperwork right here, Miss Phon. Just sign the waiver and leave the card," he said.

Her blood boiled at the pronunciation of her name, so similar to Trufante's. If she was going to continue field work, she might need to consider an alias that rednecks could pronounce, she thought as she mindlessly filled out her name and address on the form. The big Cajun drifted in beside her.

It would be easy enough to erase the computer trail, but the physical form and having to leave the credit card were troubling. She smiled, "Do we really need all this paperwork?" she asked and slid a hundred dollar bill across the counter.

"We can work with you there," he grabbed the bill and smiled, his grin a stark contrast to Trufante's, "but I gotta say, the two of you are one unlikely couple."

"You know what they say - opposites attract." She giggled and put her arm around the Cajun. He finally reached behind him and took a set of keys off a hook on the pegboard. "Either of you drive one of these before?"

"I'm from the bayou. Been playin' chicken with these bad boys since I was knee-high to a 'gator's back," Trufante said.

She had assumed correctly that he could run the airboat, basing her opinion solely on the inherent redneck factor. They followed the man to the dock where a half dozen boats were tied off. Trufante grabbed a line, pulling the boat towards him. He got on, held the boat close to the dock for her and extended a hand. She crossed the dock but one of her heels caught in the gap between the boards. Mac's phone flew out of her pocket, almost landing in the water, and she cursed. After extracting the heel, she remembered the messenger bag was still in the car. "Just a second."

"Wait," Trufante said. "You're going to break an ankle in those shoes, end up in the 'glades as 'gator bait. Let me have those."

Warily, she took off the shoes and handed them to him. One at a time he snapped the heels and handed them back. Straw cowboy hat was laughing and she put them back on. She scooped the phone off the dock and passed it to Trufante and waddled back to the car, trying to get a feel for the new footwear, grabbed the bag, and made a mental note to contact the office and have the vehicle picked up.

The roar from the motor startled her and she felt the backdraft from the huge propeller. The airboat reminded her more of an amusement park ride than a boat, not that she would be comfortable on anything short of a cruise ship. In all truth, she was more at ease in a cool, dark room staring at computer monitors, than out in the field, and The Everglades were WAY out in the field.

Steeling herself, she approached the boat and stared at the craft. The huge propeller jiggled inside the steel cage as the motor idled, just waiting for the signal to start spinning at mind-boggling revolutions that would propel the narrow, flat-bottomed boat at close to sixty mph.

Straw cowboy hat extended his hand again. She took it and boarded, acknowledging she was better for the footwear modification. There were four seats, two abreast. She went to what would be the passenger seat and buckled herself in, clutching her bag to her chest. The man grinned, grossing her out as he rubbed against her to make sure the belt was secure. Trufante sat in the driver's seat, gripping the stick between them, a wild grin on his face.

The man jumped onto the dock, untied the line and tossed it onto the deck of the boat. With a quick kick from his cowboy boot, the boat floated backwards into the canal. Trufante wasted no time and engaged the throttle, moving the boat forward.

"Ready, little lady?" he yelled over the roar of the engine.

"Wait," she screamed. "Aren't there life jackets?"

Trufante bent down, reached into a hold set in the deck, and withdrew an orange life vest which she placed over her head and tied. She carefully took out the tablet from her bag and clutched it tightly with both hands, wishing she had brought the military-grade case with it. The GPS map opened and she pointed towards the south. "There."

He wasted no time. The boat swerved as the propeller started to spin only six feet behind her. The noise was deafening. She gripped the base of the seat with her legs while holding the tablet in a death grip. The boat straightened as he accelerated and she could feel the water barely kissing the hull as they approached fifty mph. Ignoring the scenery, she called directions and focused on the green dot on the screen that marked their position. The boat flew through the maze of sawgrass.

Without the GPS, she would be totally lost, and even with it, everything looked the same. When she finally looked up, sawgrass and water surrounded them, except for the narrow channels that acted like roads through the field of grass. They reached the main canal and she was almost thrown from her seat as he banked the boat hard to the right without slowing.

The detention facility appeared in the distance, impossible to miss. It was the only building for miles. She could see the pick-up point ahead, but there was no one there.

SEVENTEEN

They ran down the hallway and reached the exit door. Mac pulled Armando into a shallow alcove and looked through the small window. Men and vehicles moved like ants across the yard chasing invisible threats. He brought his attention back to Armando and tried the carbon fiber key in the handcuffs encircling his wrists, figuring it would be better to lose a few minutes here, where it was relatively safe, than have his motion restricted when they went to climb the fence. His hands shook as he inserted the key in the lock and tried to turn it. It bound, and he twisted the thin key, easy at first, but then he heard a sound by the door and tried to free it. It snapped in half. He looked the man in the eyes, shrugged and stuck the broken piece in his pocket. He was about to open the door and move outside when he looked through the window and saw a group of men dressed in riot gear coming towards them. He pulled Armando back into the alcove and peered out the door, waiting for the men to pass.

Armando held the cuffs up with a pleading look on his face, but there was nothing Mac could do. The alarms were still sounding when he pushed open the exit door, adding one more siren to the confusion, and entered the yard. Armando followed him. He stayed close to the building, using it for cover. They reached the corner, looked across to the holding pond, and saw the double row of twelve-foot high fences. A single-story utility building interrupted the chain-link barriers topped with a swirl of razor wire on top. Fifty yards on the other side of the building, Mac saw the section of fence Alicia had promised to decommission.

He looked at the Cuban, whose eyes were wide with fear, raised his eyebrows to try and reassure him, and breathed deeply while he waited for him to acknowledge he was ready. Armando nodded and they sprinted across the yard to the fence. Mac ran to the building, using it for cover as they moved towards the single fence on the other side. They reached it unobserved. He hesitated for a second, his fingers inches from the links. It was up to Alicia now. If she failed to disable the electric fence, in seconds he would be twitching on the ground.

A whistle blasted in the distance. He feared they had been spotted. Without a second thought, he grabbed the fence, half expecting to be shocked, and started to climb. He reached the top and swung one leg over, then the other. Armando was behind him, moving slowly, his hands together, limited by the handcuffs. Mac climbed halfway down and jumped to the ground. He looked up and watched Armando struggle to get over the top. He would have to free his hands but it would have to wait. He saw a truck racing towards them.

"Hurry. I'll catch you," he called out, before he realized the man couldn't understand him. Armando jumped and landed in a crouch. The two men found themselves in a grassy area with another smaller fence separating them from the water. Mac hadn't expected this, but there was no other way out. They ran to the fence and he stopped short.

Alicia had said nothing about this fence and he suspected current was running through it. He needed something to protect them from the charge running through the wire. His gaze moved to Armando's restraints. There was no way he was getting over the obstacle with steel hanging from him. He needed to insulate the man from the metal. He took off his t-shirt, tore it into strips, reached for Armando's hands and wove the cotton material in and out of the bracelets, careful to protect the skin.

The Cuban resisted at first, but men were yelling and an engine could be heard moving closer. Armando froze, staring at the pursuit, but Mac pushed him forward, urging him on. With no choice, Armando grabbed the fence. Mac quickly wrapped his own hands and was about to grab the first links when something whizzed by his head. They would be target practice going over the barrier, but the safety of the water on the other side forced him to start climbing. Another bullet passed by. He felt something sting his butt. It burned, but he was still able to climb. He reached the ground and realized they were shooting rubber bullets.

Armando landed beside him and the men took off to the waiting water. Guards were screaming behind them. They reached the edge and dove into the scum-covered pond.

He started to swim towards the brush-lined shore, but stopped and turned when he saw Armando struggling behind him. Unable to use his hands the man struggled to keep his head above water. Mac reached him, grabbed his collar and rolled him on his back. With one arm around Armando he turned on his side and kicked hard towards the shore. He dared a glance at their pursuers. The men were running parallel to the fence, unable or unwilling to climb it.

They were safe until the guards could regroup. He hoped he could cross the brush and reach the canal before they were able to mobilize and follow. Any second he expected to hear the off-road vehicles needed to pursue them.

Armando was able to keep his pace as they ran over the scrub and sand, his restraints not a factor. They reached a trail and turned onto it, the hard packed terrain allowing them to sprint. Ahead, Mac could see the road that ran a hundred yards away from the canal. He tried to even his breath and run faster. In the distance he heard the sound of several engines whine and suspected the guards were near, the ATVs they used would be on them in seconds. He ran faster.

They crossed the road and stopped short of the empty canal. There was no sign of Trufante. He looked around for another escape route, and started to run back into the brush. With Armando on his heels, he veered towards the palmettos, when he heard the distinctive sound of an airboat. He looked back and saw two ATV's, their rifle racks already visible as they sped towards them. With nowhere else to go, they ran to the canal. He could just see Trufante's grin beaming from the driver's seat and the orange-clad figure of the girl clutching her bag next to him. His relief was short-lived when another rubber bullet hit his thigh, bringing him to the ground. He tried to get up but the bullet had temporarily crippled him. Armando helped him to his feet. Together both men stumbled into the water, yelling in Spanish and English for the Cajun to hurry.

The boat looked like it was going to run them over, but at the last second, Trufante cut the engine to an idle, hopped from the driver's seat to the bow and hauled Armando on board. Mac felt hands grab him, reached for the low gunwales of the boat and tried to board. He was breathless and his leg was useless, numbed by the shot. Finally, aided by

Trufante, he slithered onto the steel deck.

"Go!" he yelled to the Cajun. He winced as bullets hit the steel cage guarding the propeller. One bullet catching a blade in the right spot could cripple the boat. Trufante hopped back in the driver's seat and immediately revved the engine. Several long seconds later, the boat moved. Mac clung to the metal sides, pinned to the deck and breathing heavily as the boat quickly gained speed. He looked over at Armando who was beside him grasping the base of a chair.

Mac looked back at the shore and saw the men standing by the ATVs, unable to follow. One was on a radio and Mac suspected a helicopter was being called in. Fighting the force of the fifty-mile-an-hour wind caused by the forward progress of the boat, he rose to his knees and crawled back to Alicia.

"We've got to get to cover," he yelled over the engine roar. "You got that map?"

She looked back at him. He saw panic in her eyes. Reaching up, he grabbed the tablet from her and watched her move her hands to the rails of the seat. The grip was tight enough that he could see the muscles bulging in her arms. Leaning back against the seat base, he examined the device. He had never used one, but it looked like the screen of his phone. The screen lit up when he pushed the power button and he slid under the seat to avoid the glare of the sun. He pushed the map icon and waited while the screen shifted to show the red dot marking their location. Spreading his fingers on the screen, he zoomed out and panned towards the south, looking for an exit from the canal.

The screen confirmed his fears that they were landlocked. He looked up at the embankments on each side of the man-made canal, a boundary between the residential subdivisions on the left and the wilds of The Everglades on the right. Glancing back at the map, he followed the course of the canal all the way to where it crossed South Dixie Highway near Florida City and emptied into Manatee Bay. There was no way, even traveling at this speed, they could escape through the canal. Even if they were not worthy of a helicopter to chase them, the canal crossed too many roads. It would be easy to set up officers at the bridges to stop them. The only way out was through the back country, the huge expanse of sawgrass and swamp, littered with small islands identified by the clumps of cypress trees that had hidden smugglers and criminals for centuries.

Mac slid the tablet back into Alicia's bag, fought his way to his feet, grabbing the side rail for support. The woman was oblivious to their plight, the muscles in her arms trembling from her hold on the seat, a look of pure terror on her face. He reached for the rail behind her, pulled himself up and slid into the empty seat behind Trufante. He was eye-level with the top of the berm now and had to stand to see over it.

Sawgrass stretched as far as he could see, invisible from this angle was the water he knew lay beneath. The only way over was to jump the embankment. He suspected it could be done and leaned forward to tell Trufante what he wanted. Just as he sat back, he heard a helicopter behind them.

"Now!" he yelled.

Trufante wasted no time. He turned the stick towards the bank and accelerated. The boat swerved and stalled, throwing them forward when it hit the berm.

"More speed!" Mac called.

Trufante steered back to the center of the canal and accelerated. They were moving faster, the engine whining at its top speed. Mac looked over at Alicia, frozen in place, and Armando, still clutching the deck. A quick look overhead and he knew this was the only chance they would get.

Trufante took a different angle, learning from the last try that a head-on approach was not going to work. The starboard corner hit ground and this time the boat's momentum lifted it onto land. The flat hull moved slowly up the rise, juking every time it hit small roots and rocks. Mac felt the engine strain as the boat reached the crest, but he was looking down on the vast expanse of sawgrass. The boat slid easily, picking up speed on the downhill side, and the bow crashed into the water, sending a wave onto them. The boat plowed through the sharp grass, that moved and then sprung back in place, concealing their trail. He looked up. The helicopter veered away, not having the range to chase them through the wilderness.

EIGHTEEN

Trufante had to slow the boat as the ground below them changed. Sawgrass had yielded to scrub and he was forced to navigate around small islands scattered through the swamp.

Mac heard Alicia yell something; her voice lost to the wind. He bumped Trufante and raised a clenched fist, signaling him to stop. The helicopter had turned back several minutes ago and they were out of immediate danger. He suspected the authorities would be watching exit points from the area and would be patient letting the swamp do their work for them. The inhospitable ground had nothing to offer. There was no fresh water; the once pristine wilderness was brackish or polluted with fertilizers. Food was hard to come by unless you were a trained hunter after 'gators, snakes, deer, or the rare panther. With no weapon or fishing gear they had no chance.

The boat skidded to a stop, the engine behind them still loud as it idled, but they were able to hear each other.

"Ain't no potties out here," Trufante said.

She glared at him, took the tablet from her bag and turned it on. "We are lost."

"Shit, honey, there's no lost out here, just north, south, east and west. Any of those directions get you back to civilization; some are just further than others."

She pulled the tablet from her bag and focused on the screen.

"How are you getting a signal out here?" Mac asked.

"Satellites," she answered without looking up. But I can't get any detail."

"That's because there isn't any. Every time it rains the terrain changes." He looked ahead, "We are heading south by southwest: should exit this mess in Florida Bay. A lot of stuff won't show on that." The dangerous shallows of Florida Bay were more difficult to navigate than the barren Everglades.

Armando rose from the deck, moved to the empty seat in front of Trufante, and said something in Spanish.

"He thanks you for helping him," Alicia interpreted. She reached into her hair, pulled two bobby pins out, and asked him to hold out his hands. Seconds later, the handcuffs clattered on the metal deck.

He rubbed his hands together, smiling.

"Yo, Chi-fon. Now that's some useful shit," Trufante said. She replaced the pins in her hair. "Didn't know you could do that with plain old bobby pins."

She looked at him and mimicked his accent. "Those ain't no over-the-counter pins. That's top-secret CIA shit." They all laughed, breaking the tension.

"Head out?" Trufante asked.

Mac nodded and pointed the direction he wanted them to go. Trufante pushed one of the levers forwards and the boat vibrated as the propeller spun up. They headed towards the bay. Mac figured they were less than an hour out and started to plan how to get Armando back into Cuba. The island was only one hundred and eighty miles away: an hour in a plane, three hours by car, five in a fast boat. There was no road, and the airboat would be useless once they left the shallows of Florida Bay.

The landscape changed again and Trufante accelerated now that he was sure they had enough water under the boat. The sawgrass was gone, yielding to small mangrove islands with open water between them. The bay was close. Mac struggled to see the landscape ahead and decided on a point of land. Getting into the bay would be tricky. He had never been through here, but had researched several fishing trips to The Ten Thousand Islands to the west and remembered a long strip of land separating The Everglades from the bay to the east. He motioned to Trufante to steer west where he knew the water emptied into the bay.

The landscape changed again a few minutes later and they found themselves on a shallow flat, with what he thought looked like a road ahead. He signaled Trufante to the south, away from the road. Minutes later they were in open water, the sand bottom only inches below the hull. Several small Keys lay ahead and Mac pointed to the southeast, in the direction of Islamorada.

Twenty minutes later, they had cleared the land barrier and were part way along a chain of small islands when the engine sputtered. Trufante looked at him and shook his head. The engine revved again and then died. "Steer towards land while we still have some momentum," Mac said. His voice seemed loud without the roar of the engine behind him.

Trufante turned towards the closest Key, goosing every inch of forward progress they could gain, but the boat coasted to a stop a hundred yards from shore. Mac turned to the engine and stared at it, wondering where to start troubleshooting, when something zipped by his head. There had been no gunshot and he ignored it. Seconds later another projectile hit the cage and bounced to the deck. Mac bent over, picked it up and held it out for the others to see.

"What the heck - a golf ball?" Trufante said as another ball shot over their heads.

Confused, they looked at the island where the balls were coming from and saw several figures standing on the shore. Mac reached for the single oar strapped to the gunwale and started to paddle towards land. The incoming balls had stopped. The figures huddled together, obviously planning. He had no choice but to seek their benevolence. They were close enough to see the three unshaven and dirty men; holding beers, one leaning on a golf club.

"Can we get a hand?" he called out as they approached.

The man with the golf club just stared at them. "You got my balls?"

Mac tossed the single ball to him. "Engine died." He was starting to worry now, and noticed a rifle behind the leg of one of the men. All three were staring at Alicia.

"That's some exotic shit you got there," one of the men said. "We'd be happy to help." They giggled.

Mac knew the stories about the backwaters of the bay and wished he had a gun. Just miles from Miami, things were very different here. The area was lawless, too large and desolate for law enforcement to patrol. He looked around but there was nowhere else to go. Powerless, the clock to save Mel ticking in his head, he knew he would have to make the best of it, and paddled the remaining few feet to land.

One of the men entered the water, took the dock line from the deck and pulled the boat onto the sandy shore. The men surrounded them.

"Vance is the name," the man with the golf club said.

"Bugger Vance," one of the men chuckled. The third laughed at the joke. "Thinks he's a pro golfer like that dude in the movie."

Vance smacked him in the side of the head and the group fell silent. He picked up the manacles from the deck. "Looks like y'all got some 'splaining to do."

Mac hoped their outlaw status would help gain some sympathy. "Broke him out."

"Strange bunch," Vance said. He tossed the restraints on shore and moved towards Alicia. "Two white boys, a Cuban and a gook. Not the usual company we see come through here. Maybe y'all oughta get off the boat and tell us what you're running from." He leered at Alicia, who clung to the life jacket.

They followed the men to a clearing with a fire pit and several chairs. Mac scanned the brush for their boat or an escape path, but the shack had been placed in dense brush on purpose. The smell of chemicals was in the air. He suspected their purpose was not recreation.

Vance reached into a cooler and pulled out a beer. "Why don't y'all sit down," he said and indicated a group of camp chairs by the fire.

Mac smelt the air again and started putting things together. The only thing he could do was cooperate, but he was getting more uncomfortable by the minute, and searched for any weapon or escape option he could find. Following directions, at least for now, he motioned the group towards the chairs.

He sat and looked at the man in a dirty, sleeveless t-shirt and torn camo shorts, his golf club extended in front of him like he was lining up a putt. The other men were behind them. Before he could react, he felt the barnacles on the crab trap line scrape his skin as they tossed it over him and pulled. He fell from the chair and they wrapped him, the abrasive line tearing open scabs from his partially healed cuts. He looked at Trufante and Armando, struggling against their restraints. Alicia remained in the chair, arms crossed protectively across the life jacket still strapped to her chest, tears streaming down her face as Vance approached her.

NINETEEN

Norm walked along the beach making a list in his head. He tried Alicia's number, cursed as again it went to voicemail and hung up. A message or text would leave a trail. A missed call to an operator under his control would look normal if his plan fell apart and there was an investigation. She would see the call and know he was looking for her. Activity along the path picked up as he walked, the barely-clothed joggers and rollerbladers momentarily distracting him.

Getting Travis and Armando back in time for the ferry was paramount. He walked past several hotels and turned into the main airport entrance and followed the sign for Key West Seaplane Adventures.

He waited while the woman behind the counter booked a flight to the Dry Tortugas, the charter company's specialty. Finally she completed the reservation, hung up and acknowledged him.

"Going to Fort Jefferson?" she asked.

He dug into his pants' pockets for his wallet and remembered it was gone, but found a crumpled business card in a front pocket, removed it and pushed it across the counter. "Looking for a private charter for later today."

She thumbed the card. "You're going to have to put a deposit. Where is your destination?"

"Have to pick up some folks, and then to Key West, somewhere between here and Miami."

"That's a little vague." She pulled out a calculator and started to punch numbers.

His patience was waning. "It's on the government. Just call the number on the card; they'll authorize the expense."

"No offense, but we run a tight operation here - no credit." She handed the business card back to him.

His credentials were gone along with his wallet, cash and credit cards. The bump on his head started pounding again.

He handed her the card back. "This is official business. I'll expect the plane standing by," he said, puffing his chest out. He realized what he must look like and ran his fingers through his hair.

"Cash or credit card only," she said and casually answered the phone.

He felt ignored. "Have it ready. I'll be back." He tried not to sound like the terminator. He left the office and started to jog out of the airport, reaching a full run by the time he made the main road, cursing every step.

***

A swarm of tiny bugs swirled around Mac's head and he had to force his eyes open as the near invisible insects attacked. He squirmed in the sand for a better vantage point of the camp and saw the men standing around Alicia. Something moved by his side and he jerked, thinking it was one of the myriad of bugs or snakes common here, but he heard a grunt and felt a hand on his back. Fingers pried at the restraints and he heard Trufante whisper something, but the men were talking louder and he couldn't understand.

"Come on, Bugger. Let's have some fun."

He heard a slap and Vance whined, "I told you to stop calling me that. Now take Junior here and go finish the batch. From the look of this group, they're running from something, and we don't need no company with that shit cooking."

Mac saw the two men walk away and sniffed the air trying to place the smell. He'd thought at first it was acetone, but realized it was ether. He looked at Bugger, who leered over Alicia, his hand moving toward her face.

"Hey, let us go and we won't turn you in," he said trying to distract him.

Boots kicked sand in his face as Bugger came towards him and he looked up at the rotting teeth just before the man wound up and swung the golf club, falling slightly off balance before landing a blow to Mac's side. Even off balance, the blow hurt and he held back a scream. Had the tweeker been sober, the stroke might have done serious damage, but he was dealing with meth heads. These men had obviously not learned the lesson from *Scarface*: the first rule of dealing was to not use your own shit.

"Y'all are dead once my boys finish this batch. I'd do it now, but I gotta play a few holes, and then I promised them we'd share the girl around first." He turned towards her. "Besides, can't afford no gunshots till we're ready to go."

Mac sat helpless as Bugger grabbed Alicia's bound hands and lifted her from the chair. Ignoring her screams, he pushed her forwards towards an opening in the brush.

"Now act nice, little girl." He laughed and pushed her onto the narrow trail leading out of sight.

They were alone now and Mac turned to Trufante. "Can you work them loose?" He felt fingers working the restraints.

"Old boys tied them good, and the barnacles ain't helping. Nasty ass line."

Mac looked around for anything that could help and saw Armando slithering towards the chairs. He watched as he moved towards the fire pit and knocked his legs against a tree stump used for a table. A glass pipe fell from the stump and he grabbed it in his mouth, gagging at the taste, but secured it and slid towards them.

"Nice," Mac said. He took the pipe from Armando's teeth. "Tru, can you find something to break it?"

They froze as a man entered the clearing. He looked at the stump and started searching the area around it. Mac could tell he was becoming anxious by his body language as he widened the search, finally focussing on the pipe in Mac's hands.

"Y'all should have said you wanted to get high. We could use you to test the batch. Bugger usually makes me do it, but hell, better you than me." He reached for the pipe. "You never know when Bugger has a few bad holes how the batch is gonna come out."

Mac dropped the pipe and the man bent over to retrieve it. With all the power he had left, he spun his body and struck him with his legs. The man lost his balance but stayed on his feet. He stumbled away and dug a container from his pocket, filled the bowl and lit it. Mac watched him inhale and hold the smoke until he almost gagged. Before he released the drug from his lungs, he crossed to Mac and blew it in his face. Mac was able to hold his breath, but the man relit the pipe and inhaled again. This time, before he blew the smoke into Mac's face, he kicked him in the stomach, forcing the air from his lungs. Mac had no choice but to breathe in the evil vapor.

He choked on the acrid fumes, gagged, and accidentally inhaled more. The smoke stung his lungs and he tried to repel it, but gagged again and inhaled another breath.

"Never know if we got us a good batch or not. Old Bugger was smacking those balls around this morning. Should be a good one." He put the pipe back to his mouth and sucked hard.

Mac was prepared this time and did his best to hold his breath until the smoke dissipated. The cloud hung in the humid air; the only benefit was it cleared the bugs out. The man was about to repeat the process when they heard a scream.

"Shit, gotta go or I'll miss the fun."

Mac's heart was slamming in his chest and he feared the chemicals were working. Another scream and he searched frantically for anything to free them. The small knife he had found on the sailboat had been confiscated in Krome, but the memory moved his focus to his pocket and he felt the small piece of carbon fiber, the broken handcuff key.

"Tru, in my pocket." He faced him. "There's half the key."

"What's a key going to do?" the Cajun asked.

"Just do it," Mac said, and thrust his groin uncomfortably close to Trufante's bound hands. He felt fingers enter the pocket and the key move. "That's it."

Trufante worked the broken key out of Mac's pants and stared at the splintered end. He took it and maneuvered into a position to work the restraints. Another scream, this time a man, came from the brush.

"Hurry up. Something bad is going down," he said. Two men could be heard yelling at each other. He couldn't make out the words, but he had a good idea what they were fighting about. Something crashed just as his bonds released. With the use of both hands, he fumbled with the knots holding Trufante and Armando tossing the nasty rope to the side.

The three men edged down the trail, the sound of a fight directly ahead of them. As long as the tweekers were fighting between themselves, there was a better chance Alicia was unharmed. They reached the edge of the clearing where several tables were set up with beakers and Bunsen burners like a primitive chemistry class. Two men were rolling in the dirt, Bugger standing over them. He yelled something to encourage them to continue and went into the shack

Mac gave a signal for the others to wait. He went to the table, grabbed a beaker full of clear liquid, ran to the shack and entered the dark room just as Alicia screamed. He heard a slap, but had to wait for his eyes to adjust to the darkness before he could act. He had no idea what was in the container, but he knew it was bad.

"Bugger!" he yelled, waiting for his eyes to adjust to the dim light. He could see the man lurching over the bed. Vance turned, about to move on Mac, when he tripped. Mac flung the liquid in his face and went for Alicia. Bugger grabbed for his eyes and screamed.

Mac led her from the hut and ran to Trufante and Armando. Bugger ran from the shack and stumbled into the table, knocking it onto its side.

"Hurry up!" Mac pushed the group forward. He knew there were volatile chemicals mixing together. They raced forward. He chanced a look back. A beaker lay overturned by one of the burners, its contents burning blue as it spread across the ground. Mac ran after his group, a loud whoosh behind him and the clearing ignited. They felt the heat from the blast on their backs. Something else blew, the concussion from the explosion knocking them to the ground. Fire burned around them as the liquid, spread by the explosion, carried the flaming fuel to anything that could burn.

"The other side. They have to have a boat," Mac yelled.

They ran to the water, skirting the shoreline until they could see the engine of a skiff sticking from the brush. Mac raced towards the boat. The fire was burning closer. If it reached the fuel tank, they would be stranded in the inferno.

Armando beat him to the boat and both men struggled to pull it into the water just as the flames kissed the bow. Mac jumped in and frantically pulled the starter cord. Flames burned on the water and he pulled again. Armando kept pushing the boat towards deeper water, but the flames came greedily towards them as if they knew more fuel lay ahead.

Mac looked back and saw Alicia, knee deep in the water, frozen in place. The flames were skirting around her, small droplets of fire approaching as the chemicals surfed the small waves. She hugged her life jacket with her arms and screamed.

"Tru!" Mac yelled towards the shore at the Cajun striding towards the boat. "Start this piece of crap and circle back." He didn't wait for an answer. Alicia was in a total panic less than fifty feet away. The water was only a few feet deep. He took a deep breath and dove into the shallows. His only chance of reaching her safely was to stay submerged. Mac squinted, eyes burning from the salt water, the orange glow on the surface above. Bubbles escaped his lips as he metered out his breath in an attempt to stay calm and reach the girl. He knew from years of experience never to empty his lungs. Devoid of air, the body would react by gagging and he could drown - or burn.

He saw her legs underwater, dancing frantically. Without knowing if the fire had reached her, he blew the last of the breath from his lungs and surged forward, surfacing beside her. He felt the heat of the fire by his face and took in a huge breath.

"Breath!" he yelled at her, and without waiting for an answer, took one last breath and hauled her under the surface just as the flames found the vacant spot. She was dead weight made worse by the buoyancy of the life jacket, but at least she was not fighting him as he kicked towards deeper water. Just as the last bubbles left his mouth, he heard the sound of an outboard. He rolled his head back and looked at the surface. Flames were still visible. He could only hope they had lost their intensity as the chemicals burned off. They surfaced and he looked for the boat, spinning almost completely around before he saw the bow coming towards them. He feared they were out of time as flames kissed his face and found Alicia's life vest. Alone, he would have gone under to protect himself, but he glanced at the girl. She was barely conscious and he doubted she could breathe on her own. With his arm around her neck in a rescue hold, he sidestroked towards a small patch of water where the flames had burned off.

TWENTY

Trufante was in the stern, the smile back on his face while he steered the old metal skiff from the motor. The aluminum hull was about fourteen feet long, dinged and abused. A forty horsepower Evinrude engine from another decade was bolted on the transom. There were no controls: steering and throttle were all on the engine itself.

Mac looked forward at Armando, who stared at the water ahead as if he was wondering what tragedy awaited them now. The man had seen the worst side of America in less than a week. Alicia was curled up on the deck, still clutching her life jacket. The sobbing had decreased to an infrequent chest heave, but she was not responsive when he asked her questions. There was not much he could do for her until they reached land. The experience of Bugger Vance and his meth lab would likely stay with her for a while. They were the kind of wounds time healed slowly.

He looked back at the plume of black smoke rising from the island, the chemical-induced flames had burned fast and hot but were now reduced to a smolder. Daylight faded and they dropped the anchor once out of sight of the island. There was nowhere to go in the dark. Mac kept watch, unable to sleep with the drugs running through him.

They were all awake when the sun lit the horizon. Trufante started the engine and they headed for the mainland. Mac navigated by dead reckoning, using what he knew of the area, and the sliver of sun just creeping into view, to establish a course. The Keys lay to the east and he pointed Trufante at the chain of islands somewhere over the horizon. With no electronics, he tried to recall charts he had seen and figured they were still at least ten miles from Key Largo. The light blue water below the boat told him how shallow the bay was, but the boat only drew a foot or so, and unless they struck a coral head, they would be fine.

The mood of the group lightened as the sun climbed into the sky. Mullet jumped nearby, taunting the birds that circled overhead, hunting the bounty below the water. Occasionally a bigger splash indicated a predator attacking bait from below, or one of the birds grabbing a baitfish from above.

Alicia stirred and lifted her head. "Where are we going?"

She looked ragged, her mascara tracing the lines from her tears. Mac took his hand and draped it over the boat, catching some water in his palm. She flinched when he reached for her face, but relaxed as he wiped the black streaks from her cheeks.

"Should be in Key Largo in about an hour; figured we'd slide into one of the coves there and work things out." He looked down at the water and guessed their speed at ten knots. The days had blurred together and he had to pause to think if it was Friday morning, calculating he had a day and a half, at best, to get Armando home before Davies could inflict his will on Mel. "You trust that boss of yours?" Mac asked Alicia. It might have been her condition, but her pause gave a clear indication that maybe she didn't. He had completed phase one of the promise and gotten Armando out of Krome. It was time to see what the CIA man was made of, and if he could deliver his boat as promised.

"Sure. His word is good." She paused again and her face tightened. "I'm just not so sure of his motivations."

The first small Key drifted by to port. Mac checked their bearing against the sun to make sure Trufante remained on course, and watched the color of the bottom to estimate the depth. He called out a slight correction and faced her again. "You're the Cuba expert. Tell me what you're thinking." He knew she was vulnerable right now, but the information could be critical. If she had doubts, he needed to know them.

"There are some things that are not making sense," she started.

He gave her a reassuring look, but remained quiet. If she was going to talk, it needed to be her own choice.

She drew a deep breath and began. "OK, so...I have to give you some background first. None of this is in the news."

Mac leaned forward, sure the dam was about to burst.

She spoke quickly. "It's China. Chinese politics are very complicated. They are not interested in immediate gratification, as we are. Their foreign policy is designed to win by attrition, wear down the opponent over time. Since the Soviet bloc broke up in the eighties, they have been working to gain a foothold into the Americas. Cuba has two choices; they had three, but since Chavez died, Venezuela is out of the picture. They need the help of either the United States or China, the only countries with the resources to bring them into the twenty-first century. The government is split into two factions: one supporting patience and waiting for the US to come around, the other more interested in the cash that China is willing to dump in the country right now. With the president easing trade restrictions, the pro-US faction is happy, but the Chinese, seeing their plans about to unfurl, are getting nervous."

Mac absorbed what she was saying. She was right. He had no idea China was a player, but it all made sense. "What does this have to do with Armando?"

She was about to speak when the boat jerked forward and the engine changed pitch. The lower unit snapped back and lifted out of the water. They stared at each other, fearing they were stranded again, but the propeller fell back into the water and they resumed their course. Mac checked the horizon, the thin land mass a faint blur. A stern look back at Trufante and he turned to Alicia, waiting for her to continue.

"Armando Choy, his grandfather," She looked over at the Cuban resting against the gunwale, "Was instrumental, along with a surprising number of Chinese, in Castro's revolution. The Chinese faction remained strong in the government, often assimilating, as his father did, by marrying local women, and in some cases changing their names - in this case from Choy to Cruz." She stopped. "Ok, that's the background."

They stared at the horizon, the land mass rising from the water as they approached. Mac knew he had to keep her talking. Once they reached land, her attention would be diverted. He felt awkward, needing to reassure her. He looked her in the eye and nodded.

She breathed in again. "It's more about money now, but some of the old guard, especially the Chinese, are still driven by ideology. For their goals, at least for now, Cuba can remain in the fifties. The closer they move to the United States, and the evils of the internet and social media, their grasp on the island weakens. There are some that would do anything to keep it that way."

"What would *anything* mean?" Mac asked.

She looked down at the deck as if she was confessing, "There has been chatter lately about an EMP being set off, but I think that is too drastic. I've been digging and heard some rumors, but since the Clinton's cut the intelligence agents in the field, we have little information."

The boat lurched again, this time tilting to a forty-five degree angle as it struck a shoal. "Can't you drive?" Mac yelled back at Trufante, and then turned back to Alicia, but he knew he had lost her.

"The glare; I can't see," Trufante yelled back.

Mac looked ahead and tried to read the water, but with the angle of the sun, it was impossible. They were close to land and he concentrated on their surroundings, trying to pinpoint their position. A long stretch of barren land lay to the port side and a more developed area was ahead. He pointed towards the tallest building and racked his brain, trying to remember the area.

"Blackwater Sound to the left," he called back to Trufante, "Key Largo ahead." He stood and scanned the horizon, the letters EMP resounding in his head. From the bow, he studied the water. Using his outstretched arm like a weather vane, he guided Trufante to the lee side of a small Key about a mile off the mainland. Trufante cut the engine. Mac leaned forward and tossed the anchor line.

"Can you get a signal on that tablet of yours?" he asked.

Alicia released the grip on his arm and looked for her bag. "My bag is on the airboat."

Mac wondered how he was going to contact Norm now, and then remembered Alicia had the phone. He prayed it still worked after their swim. "How about your boss's phone?"

Alicia looked confused. "I don't know———"

"You mean this?" Trufante slid his hand in his button-down breast pocket and triumphantly held up the phone, his trademark grin spreading across his face.

***

"Open the door." Norm pounded again. He was covered in sweat and breathing heavily after running to the house. "I'll have your ass deported!" He moved to the living room window to see if anyone was there. There was a car in the driveway, the same as last night, and he wished he had his gun. Whatever was behind the door, he would have to face it to get his credentials back.

The window opened and he faced the barrel of a gun. "Quiet, CIA man," a voice called through the screen.

"Keep the cash, OK. I just need my credit card and credentials." He lowered his voice and searched for a solution to the standoff.

"You promised me a green card if I helped you. Now you leave without even a word," the girl spat back.

"Let me in. We can talk about this," he pleaded. Without his credentials and credit card, he was powerless. It would take too long to get replacements and explaining to the local office that he'd lost them would be a bad idea.

"What? You going to promise me something again?"

"I can still get you a green card. You just have to trust me." He had no other cards to play.

The door cracked open and she motioned him inside. They stood in the living room, her hair unkempt as if he had just woken her. The shotgun covered him. He hated the scatter effect of shotguns. Rifles and handguns were so much cleaner. Her black rimmed eyes stared at him. You could tell after enough people pointed guns at you whether they had the nerve or experience to pull the trigger, and from the look on her face, she had both. He raised his hands, trying to buy some time.

She made a gesture with the barrel towards the couch. He sat and removed his phone, still unsure what to do. Just as he started to scroll through his contacts, the phone vibrated. He looked at her and she nodded.

"Travis." The number for the phone he had given him appeared on the screen. "You have the package?"

"Yeah. I want my boat back." The connection was filled with static.

"Where are you? I'll arrange transportation," he said.

"Key Largo," the voice came back. "What about my boat?"

Norm ran the numbers in his head. There was not enough time to get the boat, meet the men and get them into Cuba before the General's threat reached reality. "No time. I'm flying to meet you. I'll call for a location before we take off."

"And I'm supposed to trust you?"

Despite the gun pointed at him, he smiled. "Your girlfriend will die if we don't get this done. Surely her life is more valuable than a boat."

The line was static for a long minute. "Call me," Travis said.

Norm looked at the girl. "How about we go for a plane ride? I'll make the calls on the way."

TWENTY ONE

They had arrived in Key Largo about an hour ago, tied up to an empty dock and walked to the first food they could find. Tired and hungry, their last sustenance twenty-four hours ago, the waitress at the Waffle House had looked on in amazement as Trufante and Armando consumed plate after plate of food, eating at least two meals each. The restaurant had a WIFI connection and Mac watched Alicia stare at some of the other customers on their tablets and smartphones. She was powerless without her tablet and squirmed in her seat, barely touching her food.

Mac knew he should be starving and tired, but he sat there grinding his jaw, his stomach fluttering and pulse pounding. He had felt weird on the boat ride but had written it off as adrenaline and stared at his picked-at plate of food wondering how long it would be until the drug wore off. At least the others had gotten a meal, he thought. The phone vibrated on the table and he jumped. He answered the call, talked for a minute and disconnected. "Half an hour; we got to move." He looked at Trufante to pay the check, hoping the rednecks hadn't searched him, but the Cajun laid the cash on the table. They left the restaurant and jogged to the boat.

Twenty minutes later they were drifting with the current a quarter-mile from shore when Mac saw the opening and directed Trufante into Little Buttonwood Sound. The sun blazed high in the sky and he felt like they were baking in the uncovered metal boat. Sweat dripped from him and he ground his jaw as they waited, wondering if he could survive another minute. After years in the Keys, he was used to the heat, but the drug was taking its toll on him. Alicia had tried to comfort him, but his mind was

113

numb, focused only on Mel. He looked towards Marathon as if he could commune with her, then felt the acidic taste return to his saliva and readied himself for another rush.

Finally he heard the drone of an engine and saw a dot in the sky. The plane came into view and banked sharply. Trufante stood and waved his hands over his head to give the pilot a target, smiling when the plane wiggled its wings and approached. They watched the pontoons skid into the water and the plane landed a few hundred yards away. They waited for it to taxi towards them.

The pilot cut the port engine and stayed a safe distance from the boat until the propeller spun down. It stopped and the door opened.

Mac saw Norm duck through the opening and look towards them. "Bring it over," he called.

Trufante started the engine and idled towards the plane. They tied off and sat with several feet of water between them, staring at each other.

"You and Armando," Norm called to Mac, and then said something to Armando in Spanish.

Mac looked behind him and saw the barrel of a shotgun pointing at them. "You heard him," the girl said.

"What the hell are you doing?" Norm turned towards her.

"Just thought you could use some help," she said.

Mac stared back at Norm. "What's this all about? First you promise my boat for him." He looked at Armando. "Now there's a gun pointed at us."

"I'll take care of her," Norm said, turned his back to them and said something to the girl, who lowered the weapon.

"Come on, Travis. You want to save your girlfriend, let's go."

Mac pulled the line connecting them. The skiff brushed against the float of the plane and he held the strut while Armando got out. He followed, ducking and entered the small passenger compartment. He looked back at the boat and saw Alicia rise to board.

"Sorry, honey. That's all the room we have. You did good," Norm said to the analyst.

"But you promised me that I could be a field agent."

"Look at you. Go home; take a long bath and the rest of the day off. Heck! Take off tomorrow too."

She sat back down and clutched her arms around her chest, accepting the orders from her superior.

"What about me?" Trufante asked. "Always wanted to ride in one of those."

Norm ignored him, closed the door and turned to the pilot, who revved the starboard engine and used its power to taxi away from the skiff.

***

"Can you believe that shit?" Trufante yelled at the plane, watching it turn into the wind and pick up speed. Seconds later it was in the air and he swore he could see Norm leering at him through a window.

"I really wanted to see this through in the field," Alicia whined, feeling scorned and now embarrassed, wrapping her arms around the torn and burned life jacket.

"Well, I ain't happy about this turn of events either. My boy Mac needs me."

They stared at the plane until it disappeared into the clouds. Once it was gone they sat in silence for several minutes.

"We got to help them. I don't trust that CIA dude," Trufante said.

Alicia felt like crying. Maybe a long bath would be a good idea. She looked at the Cajun, dirty and worn out from the escape. If he looked like that, she wondered what she looked like. "I have to follow orders or I'll get fired."

"Sweetheart, you want to be a field agent, just follow my lead." He grinned at her, trying to lighten the mood. "I'll teach you some secret agent shit."

She felt a tear roll down her cheek and hoped he hadn't noticed. "I can't afford to lose my job."

"Honey, you come out guns blazing and save the day, you'll get promoted." He looked at her. "Hey, no tears, ya hear."

She clenched her jaw and fought back the moisture building in her eyes. This feeling was foreign to her. Used to sitting in a comfortable office, drinking lattes and analyzing data, she had never experienced the rush of field work, nor knew how to process it. The thought of failure was foreign to her.

"What I could really use is a drink," she said, regretting it almost immediately when she saw his face light up.

"Now you're talking," he said and started the engine.

Thankfully it started on the first pull and she could avoid his looks and conversation. She felt an emptiness deep inside her and for the first time in as long as she could remember, she felt sorry for herself. The last fifteen years of her life, and probably before that, had been a push to reach the top. Valedictorian at her private high school in the competitive Bay area of California, she went directly to Stanford, graduating in three years before heading east to do her graduate work at MIT and then multiple job offers in Silicon Valley. She had thought she wanted the riches and status of her classmates, but preferred the challenge and anonymity of the Agency. Where her peers were stressing about creating the next big thing, she was working to keep America safe to allow it to happen. Even her Dragon Mom couldn't stop her from joining.

The boat coasted to a stop and she went to wipe her eyes, but the sea breeze had already dried them. She rubbed the crust from her face and sat, glued to her seat, clinging to the life vest like it was her last friend, feeling worthless and weak as she watched Trufante jump onto the dock to tie the boat off, wishing she could do that. He extended a long arm to help her out of the boat, but she gritted her teeth and rose on her own, fighting the fear of tripping as she hopped onto the dock. One step at a time, she thought.

She flinched when he reached for her as they stood on the dock and she realized she was wobbling.

"Easy, girl. Maybe a cocktail'll help settle you."

"Thanks. Let's get that drink - on me."

"Now you're talking, little girl." He started walking towards the road.

She hurried after him, having to take two steps for each of his. There was an element of cool he carried that she needed to learn, but she suspected it came from not caring about too many outcomes, and that was foreign to her. She followed him to the street and waited while he appeared to sniff the air.

"Been a while - got to get my bearings," he said.

Across the street was a large group of buildings with signs for a marina, hotel and tiki bar. "There's a place," she said.

"That's a big-time tourista joint, but what the heck?" He walked carelessly across the road.

She stopped at the curb, paused, and looked both ways before crossing. They entered the complex and saw the bar off to the right, half-full in the early afternoon. Trufante strode directly to the tiled counter and ordered two drinks she had never heard of.

They sat and she looked around, feeling dirty and grimy, sure the yuppies hanging around the pool were all staring at her. Somehow, though, she felt tough, as if she had really done something. She looked again at the pool. How good would that feel, she thought as she put the straw to her lips and pulled hard on the colorful drink. While Trufante made mindless small talk she finished the drink and pushed it towards the bartender.

"What was that?" she asked.

"Painkiller; you should be feeling no pain soon." He took the empty glass off the bar and replaced it with a full one.

Not a drinker, she wasn't sure what he meant as she sipped the new drink.

"Slow down there, little girl," Trufante said and started on his fresh drink. "Shit'll creep up on you."

"That pool looks really good." She looked down at herself. The silk shirt was dirty and torn. White stains radiated from her armpits which she didn't dare to smell. She took another sip, the lure of the water enticing her. "I'm going in," she said, feeling no pain.

"Darn. Sounds good to me," he said, took a pull on his drink, walked to the edge of the pool, kicked off his flip flops and dove into the water, emerging on the other side, a huge smile on his face.

"But…" she hesitated, looking down at herself.

"Shit, girl; it's the Keys. Those Vegas dudes stole that *whatever happens here, stays here* shit from us."

She walked tentatively to the coping, feeling the eyes on her, not sure if she could follow through. Jumping into a bar pool in her clothes was not something Alicia Phon would do, but thinking back on the last day, and with the false courage brought by the drinks, she took a breath, held her nose and jumped in. It wasn't the same old Alicia Phon anymore.

The dirt and sweat washed off her and she looked around self-consciously to see if there was a dark cloud in the water, but the over-chlorinated pool was clear. She dunked under the water again and ran her hands through her hair, then surfaced and swam to the edge of the pool.

She pulled herself onto the lip, resting her elbows on the side allowing her body to float in the tepid water. Trufante was across the way, chatting with the other group of tourists. She glanced towards the bar, her eye catching the big screen TV. The familiar faces of the analysts caught her eye. She racked her brain, knowing the location in the background, but unable to place it.

The dull feeling left her and she sprung up from the edge of the pool and went to the bar, where she ignored the water dripping from her and stared at the screen. A knot grew in her stomach as she recognized the landscape. Fully alert, she turned to the pool.

"We have to go!" she yelled at Trufante.

TWENTY TWO

Mac stared out the window as the plane flew a course due west, parallel to the chain of islands. He glanced over the head rest at the control panel, both curious and unable to quell his captain's habit of checking things. They were flying at three thousand feet at a ground speed of 175 knots. In all his years in the Keys, after hitchhiking here twenty odd years ago, he had only taken a handful of plane trips, and even if he had flown every day, the view would never get old. Water was everywhere, its color ranging from translucent green to deep blue where the shallows blended into the Gulf. He imagined the sharks and rays cruising the flats. The white vees left by the wakes of the cruising boats were visible and he guessed where each was going. Close to Marathon, he started to pick out landmarks, pausing to think about Mel when he recognized the helipad at Fishermans Hospital. The pilot veered further to the west over open water, quickly approaching the small islands of the back country. Even from this altitude, he saw what he thought was Wood's Island off the tip of Big Pine Key, the burned house a black smudge on the landscape. He looked over at Armando across the narrow aisle of the small plane, staring out the window as well.

He switched his gaze to Norm, engrossed in his phone, oblivious to the damage he had caused below. Whatever happened in the next few days, Mac would find a way to bring him to justice. He had no choice but to cooperate for the time being. Mel's life depended on it. The unmistakable grid of Key West came into view and the pilot circled the island before cutting speed for his approach. In minutes, they were on the ground.

The pilot opened the hatch and exited the plane. He descended the small ladder and waited on the tarmac for the passengers to disembark. The group deplaned and the pilot led them to the terminal building where Norm marched the girl up to the counter and glared at her as she withdrew a credit card - his credit card - and paid the bill. Mac wondered what the deal was between the pair. She apparently held some kind of leverage over him and he wondered if it was something that could be used as a tool against the CIA man.

The glass of the terminal building vibrated from the loud boom of a bass woofer. The cab, the source of the noise, pulled up to the curb and Norm went out first. The music faded when he approached the driver. A minute later, he opened the back door for the trio to enter. He gave the driver an address and the cab pulled away from the curb. The driver, his head bopping to the silent beat, turned right on the South Roosevelt, drove past several resorts and made another right on First. As they crossed the island, Mac wondered where they were headed and almost spoke, but felt the acrid taste bleed from his glands again, and stayed quiet, not trusting his voice. The driver stayed straight, entered the causeway over Garrison Bight and continued on Palm, finally taking several quick turns and ending up at the harbor.

The streets were lined with news vans and onlookers forcing them to double park. They exited the cab and Norm pushed the girl to the driver's window. She pulled a large wad of cash from her bra, slowly pulled a bill off the roll as if it hurt her, and replaced the cash. Mac tried to figure out why they were here, but was distracted by Norm and the girl arguing. She was yelling, her Russian accent getting thicker as she argued, until Norm made a gesture towards one of the many ICE agents. A bitter scorn crossed her face as she withdrew a wallet from her back pocket and handed it to him. The ICE agent was forcing a path through the crowd when she looked away, defeat on her face, and ran.

Norm led them through the crowd at the ferry building, an open billfold, which Mac suspected were his credentials, held out in front of him. Reporters and cameramen were clustered in front of the building, grabbing people for short interviews when they tried to enter the terminal. There were women crying tears of joy, anxious children fidgeting, and men looking proud.

More ICE agents were checking papers inside the door at a brand new security kiosk and Mac had a brief, anxious moment thinking they were here for him, but relaxed when Norm said a few words, handed one of the agents his credentials and they were allowed inside.

Straight ahead, a red ribbon blocked the walkway separating the seawall and the ship; the chasm decorated with American and Cuban flags.

The crowd was pressed tightly against a rope, waiting to board, and finally a man walked to the fore with a microphone. He did some throat-clearing, then began thanking everyone for coming to the inaugural run of the new Key West to Havana ferry. He went on about the long history and new relations between the countries and finally, as the crowd's interest waned, cut the ribbon.

People slowly boarded the ferry after passing through another security station. Each was handed a small flag, which several held high above their heads, in victory, as they boarded. They were watching a small sliver of history but the machinations of politics disgusted Mac. He ground his jaw and followed Norm as he pushed his way through the crowd.

They reached the security area and another ICE agent blocked their path. Mac held his breath again, wondering why he was so paranoid. After all, he was with the CIA man. Norm and the man had a heated conversation and the agent walked away, leaving them standing to the side. A few minutes later he came back, led them to the front of the line, and they boarded the ferry. Norm apparently had some juice with the agency and they were immediately ushered to the starboard rail, away from the boarding ramp and commotion on the port side.

A band started playing the Star Spangled Banner and then another piece Mac suspected was the Cuban anthem. He felt the vibration of the deck as the motors revved and watched the crew scramble to release the dock lines. Slowly the boat inched forward.

***

"Where you thinkin' about going?" Trufante asked.

She ignored him and stared at the TV screen, the pieces falling into place. "I need a computer and internet."

"Here? Don't you need one of those hippy-ass coffee shops?"

She looked down at herself, the once expensive silk shirt wet and clinging to her body, dirty linen shorts and her heel-less shoes; she could only imagine what her hair looked like. She felt like crying.

"Hey, I've got a buddy. Maybe he can help. Works on a dive boat out of Pennekamp. Kind of a computer nerd on the side, but he likes to party."

There were no options. Her ID and credit cards had been left on the boat at the tweeker's island. "How do we find him?" she asked,

"Maybe on the reef, maybe not. You still got that phone?"

She shook her head. Everything was lost.

Trufante got the bartender's attention and placed another bill on the bar. A minute later he returned with a phone book, turned to the back bar, grabbed the phone and handed it to him. "Dial nine," the bartender said.

Alicia watched him flip through the Yellow Pages, wondering why anyone still used paper. He settled on a number, dialed, and spoke to someone.

"He's out on a charter, should be back in an hour."

"Let's go then," she said and started to leave.

"You can't go running around looking like that. There's a gift shop by the road - my treat."

She knew he was right; the fugitive look might pass over the heads of many of the tourists, but if any law-enforcement saw them, there would be questions, and she couldn't afford the time. Not wanting to go shopping with him leering over her, she held out her hand and waited while he dug in his pockets for some cash. A few minutes later she left the store feeling better in a floral print shirt and sarong wrapped around her waist.

"Chifon - lookin' fine. I was thinking more along the lines of a T-shirt."

"You gave me a hundred," she answered.

He muttered something but she was focused on the street. "Where are we going?"

"Shop's just down the road. We can walk."

Great, she thought as she felt the first beads of sweat form and cling to her new clothes. They walked a quarter mile down the sidewalk towards a building with a dive flag swinging in the breeze. Surprised when he held the door for her, she entered the humid shop, wondering why it was not air-conditioned like everything else here, but around a rack of T-shirts, she saw the back side of the building, floor-to-ceiling shuttered doors swung back, opening to a dock. She drew closer and felt the sea breeze evaporate the moisture from her skin.

Trufante walked to the counter where an unshaven, grumpy-looking man answered his questions. She walked outside and looked at the empty dock. Dive gear was neatly organized against the building but the boat was nowhere in sight.

Trufante came out and looked towards the end of the canal. "Dude in there called them on the VHF. They should be coming around any time now."

They stood together watching until finally a converted sport fisher came around the bend. The boat came closer and she heard the happy tourists talking about everything they had seen on the reef. A heavy-set man climbed down the ladder from the flybridge and started talking to the excited group. He was unshaven, his hair a nappy mess, kind of like dreadlocks, but cut short enough to stick straight out from his head. The clerk came outside and helped with the lines. She heard two girls with thick southern accents ask the man where he was going to party tonight. He grinned, tied off the boat and jumped back aboard where he pocketed a few bills from the tourists. The group gathered their gear and disembarked.

"Trufante. Son of a bitch!" he yelled and helped one of the girls off the boat. "Ladies, if my old boy Tru's in town, we'll be partying hard tonight."

Alicia felt Trufante move next to her.

"And you brought your own." The man pecked one of the girls on the cheek. "Looks like y'all will have to share me."

Alicia pushed Trufante forward.

"Yo, TJ, 'sup?" he called to the man. "Listen, I ain't here to party."

The man frowned and she wondered how he was going to be able to help her. The girls walked away giggling. His demeanor changed. "She's looking pretty serious, never mind too good looking to be hanging out with the likes of you," he said and turned to the clerk and captain. "You guys clean up the boat." He turned to Trufante, "Got to check something. We can talk upstairs."

He walked towards a set of stairs to the side of the building. They followed him upstairs into an apartment, its louvered shutters matching the open ones downstairs, but these were just for looks; the air-conditioning blasted them as they entered.

"Getting too old for this," he called to Trufante. "Beer?"

He looked at her and she shook her head, already regretting the drinks she'd had at the tiki bar. From a large, stainless steel refrigerator he pulled a bottle of water and two beers. "So, what brings you to these parts - I know you got a story."

Alicia was running out of patience. "I'm with the CIA. I need a computer and internet access." She looked towards Trufante, "He said that you could help."

"CIA?" He winked at Trufante.

TWENTY THREE

Airhorns blasted and a loud cheer came from the crowds of people on the deck and lining the shore. The brand new 107 foot ferry blasted its horn and eased away from the pier. It picked up speed, idled through the harbor, and cleared the breakwater before turning south. The pitch of the engines increased as its twin hulls came up on plane and the boat found its cruising speed. The passengers moved away from the rail, the excitement of the inaugural voyage wearing off as land disappeared. Mac stood by the rail, his stomach grumbling, hungry, the drugs finally wearing off. His head started to clear and he wondered why Norm had brought him along if he was going to be here himself. As they moved further away from Key West, he had the feeling he was moving further from his destination, instead of closer. Tomorrow he needed to be in Marathon for the ethics meeting, and going to Cuba was the wrong way. Armando was next to him, staring out to sea, a smile on his face. He knew he was going home. Norm came up behind them with a tray of food in one hand and a drink holder in the other.

"Better eat," he said. "You're looking a little better. Thought you were a goner for a while there. You were a lovely shade of green."

Mac took some tacos from the tray and sat down. Norm joined him after passing around the rest of the food. The last thing Mac wanted to do was to share a meal with the man, but he was starving now, and one way or another, he expected he would need the energy. This was not the deal, but he had little choice if he wanted to save Mel.

"This is what's going to happen," Norm said, his mouth half-full of food.

Mac turned his attention to him, fully focused on doing whatever had to be done.

"The cattle disembark first. Then there'll be a welcoming committee coming for you and Armando - some bigwig officials. I expect one of them will be his grandfather."

"What about me? You already broke your word to get my boat back," Mac said, and reached for another taco.

"There's bound to be pictures, and it's better for you to make the hand-off than me." He paused, stuffed the rest of the tortilla in his mouth and took a sip of soda. "Your girlfriend will be kept alive until you get back. I had my office let the hospital and sheriff know that you were alive and cooperating with us. They should wait for you. Who knows, maybe you'll be a hero."

"Should?"

"Unless, of course, she's declared brain dead. If that's the case, they'll pull the plug on their own."

Mac came erect and set the food down. "You never told me about that."

"Nothing you can do about it. Make the hand-off and I'll clear all channels to get you back."

The closer they came to Cuba, the more out of control he felt. The whole scheme sounded suspicious and the tacos rolled in his stomach. He left the food half-eaten, got up and started pacing. He needed to get back to Marathon and be with her. There was no doubt in his mind that Davies was there to terminate her. He'd make it look like he was all compassionate and acting in her interest, but Mac knew the man had anti-freeze running through his veins. The clock was ticking and this was all wrong.

"I'll help you with the exchange if you get me on a plane back to Key West," Mac said.

"Sure, Travis. This goes off smoothly, I'll help you. If not, you'll be dead before her."

He stared at the CIA man. "What now?"

Norm leaned close to him, "The boat is rigged to blow if we don't return Armando here to his grandfather."

Mac stared at the man, wondering how he could be so calm knowing they could be on the bottom of the sea any second. "And you let this happen? You could have told the authorities in Key West."

"This goes higher than you want to know," he said.

"There are hundreds of people at risk here and you're sitting there eating tacos. Do something," Mac pleaded.

"I am. We hand over Armando and they will disarm the bomb."

Mac tried to sort through the information but none of the pieces fit. "I have a feeling you have something to gain from all this."

"Just keep the plan the plan and everything will work out," Norm said. He stood feeling the pitch of the engines change and walked to the rail. "There's Havana, Travis."

Mac looked at the land, seeming to grow larger every second. The other passengers had seen it too and the jubilant mood embracing them earlier returned with fervor.

"Just hand over the man," Norm said sliding to the side allowing two young boys to squirm between them waving small Cuban flags.

The Havana skyline was visible now and the excitement increased. Mac looked at Armando, at the rail with the others, clearly happy to be going home.

***

Alicia stared at the dual monitors set up in what TJ had called his war room. The room was dark, painted gunmetal grey and lit only by tiny spotlights. A large screen TV covered most of one wall and framed game posters adorned the others. The glass top desk faced the big screen, looking like a command post from a high tech TV show. She sat in the chair, straight from the deck of the Starship Enterprise, and focused on the news feed streaming on one of the four monitors sitting side by side. Video of the ferry leaving the dock in Key West was on one monitor while the feed from several other cameras placed around the terminal were on two of the other screens. The final monitor directly to her right showed a chat screen, the conversation scrolling quickly down the screen. She wondered how the setup of a gamer could be better than the agency provided her. She closed the chat window when she felt the men behind her.

"Whatcha got there?" Trufante asked.

She ignored him and frantically typed a line of code. A picture appeared on the screen and she waited impatiently for the image to clarify.

"Damn, she's got ninja skills," TJ said leaning closer. "You got to show me some of that CIA voodoo."

"Can you give me some room, please. Working with this archaic equipment is hard enough without you two looking over my shoulder." She was not going to let him think he had a better setup than the CIA.

"Archaic? This is the best on the market. I rule on World of Warcraft." He reached over her shoulder, pressed a key sequence almost faster than she could recall it and the big screen TV showed a composite of all four monitors.

"You have no idea," she muttered and worked the dual track pads, wishing she had this equipment in her office. Another picture came into focus and she panned the satellite image back and forth, looking for anything out of place. The scene unfolding at the Havana dock was quite a bit more subdued than the replay of the launch on the other monitor. It looked like a step back in time, accentuated by the poor resolution of the Cuban cameras. Figures dressed in what looked like army fatigues were patrolling the line of barricades restraining the waiting people. Unlike the United States, where the media roamed freely, they were clearly corralled in one area.

"Holy mother of weaponry! That's a live shot of Havana. Me and you gotta hang out."

She smiled to herself but ignored him as an alert flashed on the screen. Nimbly she minimized the satellite view and reopened the chat screen. Text streamed faster than she could read. She scanned the interagency conversation, putting together the disparate pieces of the puzzle. The compilation program was her design, one she kept to herself. With the proper clearance an agent could access archived conversations, but this allowed real time access to any information flowing into the giant computers in Langley.

"Mac is in trouble," she said, grabbed a laser pointer off the desk and pointed to the screen, illuminating a pock-marked faced man, "General Choy is there to make the exchange. There are also rumors of a bomb that Choy has knowledge of, but at this point it's all speculation. That's where this is going: Armando for the bomb," she said and sat back. She leaned forward and started typing in a new window. She needed to get the message out, but who could she trust?

"I need to reach him," she said to the screen.

"That's some seriously trick shit you got there," TJ said. "You think if you applied that algorithm to the chat on WOW it would work?"

He was leaning over her, the ends of his short dreadlocks tickling her face. It was bothering her, but at the same time she wanted him there. "Can I text from here?"

He leaned over and clicked on an icon in the top corner of the screen. A message box opened and she started to type, thankful she had memorized the number on the phone Norm had given Mac. The number blinked on the screen and she hesitated.

"They got service in Havana?" Trufante asked.

She thought for a second and reopened the screen. Her fingers entered the number again, and the only message she could think of that wouldn't draw attention: 911. She closed the screen and looked at TJ. "What kind of range does that boat have?"

"I ain't risking my boat."

"I promise we will stay out of Cuban waters. And the agency pays well."

He took a deep sip from the beer. "You show me that shit and you're on."

***

Mac saw the tower of the Morro Castle on the left just before the narrow opening for the harbor came into view. Soon the rest of the castle was visible, the Castillo towering over the other buildings on the right. Havana had been an important port for the Spanish when they ruled the Caribbean and they had built the strongholds to protect the harbor where their treasure fleets met before attempting the dangerous crossing of the Atlantic together. Only miles from the Keys, and even Miami, the history and architecture overwhelmed him. This was stuff you expected to see in Spain, not the Caribbean. The ferry sounded a long horn blast at the tourists lining the shores and entered the Canal de Entrada. More fortifications and several parks lined the shores that had seen untold riches pass by on their way from the Americas to Spain. They rounded a slight bend and three long concrete jetties appeared on the right, their architecture from the Soviet era, a stark contrast to the elegant Spanish forts.

The captain stopped the ferry and turned, using the momentum of the boat to swing the bow away from shore, and then reversed the boat, skillfully placing the starboard side against the dock. A loud blast and the passengers started crowding the gates. The ferry was secured and Mac felt the engines stop. A group of uniformed men approached the boat. The crowd quieted on seeing the men with their automatic weapons. A well-decorated man emerged from the ranks, clearly the leader from his dress and demeanor. He walked to the closed gate and gave an order in Spanish. The gate opened and the passengers moved aside. Several soldiers followed him onto the boat.

Mac got a bad feeling and looked to where Norm was standing. The group was fifty feet away and coming right towards them when the phone vibrated. He pulled it from his pocket, his eyes never leaving the group, and flipped the screen open. He looked at the message and froze.

The head man called an order out and two soldiers separated from the group and grabbed a surprised Norm, turned him against the cabin and handcuffed him. He was led away and Mac suspected he would soon see what the infamous Cuban jails looked like. If they had no fear of the CIA man, he saw his future scratched in the rotting concrete of a cell - or worse. He had to do something.

"*Vamanos*," he whispered in Armando's ear. The armed men were approaching and he saw the look of recognition on the leader's face as he spotted them. Armando eased away from him and moved forward as if he recognized someone in the group. Mac looked around for an escape, but saw only one. He grabbed Armando and ran across the deck to the port side. The man resisted, but he took his arm and torqued it behind his back. Armando was the only card he had left. "*Vamanos*," he said louder, to make sure the man heard, and pushed him over the rail.

He followed, hit the water hard and swam for the cover of the boat as bullets entered the water around him. A blur came towards him and Armando surfaced next to him, a questioning look on his face. Mac pulled him closer just as another round of bullets was unleashed, but they were protected by the shape of the tapered hull.

Whistles sounded from above and he could hear orders being given over the screams of women and children. Bullets continued to enter the water around them and he searched desperately for a way out. The dock would be their best chance of escape, but it was on the other side of the boat. The only way to reach it was to swim around the hull, or under it. He looked at Armando, the fear clear in his eyes, and pointed under the boat. The man nodded his understanding and they both started to breathe deeply. Mac took one last breath and pivoted into the water. He kept a hand on the hull to guide him, thankful it was the maiden voyage of the boat and the bottom was free of barnacles and growth. A steady stream of bubbles exited his mouth as he reached the first keel of the catamaran and pushed up on the other side. The murky port water stung his eyes as he looked back for Armando. He thought he saw a shape coming towards him before the sting of diesel forced him to close his eyes. They breathed deeply under the protection of the hull, but the raised area between the twin hulls was visible from above and he feared they would be spotted. He took another deep breath, encouraging Armando to do the same, and submerged.

Just as his breath was exhausted, his leading hand found air and he popped to the surface. A quick look above and he saw the deck was clear, all the activity still on the other side. Armando surfaced next to him, gagging on the foul water, and Mac pointed towards the cantilevered understructure of the jetty. They breathed in again and submerged. The barnacle-covered concrete tore at his legs as Mac swam under the edge of the structure. Unable to see in the water, he popped his head to the surface and waited for his eyes to adjust to the dim light under the dock.

TWENTY FOUR

Norm lowered his head and looked away from anything that resembled a camera. He felt the sting of defeat as he was led off the boat in handcuffs. There was a massive manhunt on for Travis and Armando, but even their recovery was not going to solve his problems now. It would take every ounce of his experience and ingenuity to stay out of a Cuban prison.

The general walked ahead of them, a line of soldiers on each side clearing a path to his car. A hand reached out, opened a door and pushed Norm into the back seat. Siren blazing, the car sped off through the crowded streets. Norm was left staring at the tail lights of the general's car ahead of them. Instead of sitting in the luxury of the late fifties Rolls Royce, he was crammed in the back seat of a vintage Renault, and he used that term only because it was old. A soldier climbed into the already cramped back seat and two more got in the front. The whine of a siren began and the convoy started to move away from the pier.

The hand-off had been an unmitigated disaster, the two men jumping, and at least so far, eluding capture. Norm expected his career would be ruined. He sensed the landscape had shifted and he needed to figure out how to reach Alicia and get some quick intel. He had not expected Choy himself to be on the dock waiting for his grandson, and realized the bomb threat was not for today. Besides seeing the mission to some sort of conclusion and ensuring Travis's detention in a Cuban prison, he had a half-baked idea he could come out of this a hero, after finding the bomb. Now he was headed for ruin.

There was a risk to playing both sides, and his machinations had failed. Armando was missing and there was a bomb somewhere waiting to kill or maim hundreds of people. The blowback would be fatal to US and Cuban relations and the Chinese would strengthen their foothold in the country. He wondered if Choy ever intended to reveal the location of the bomb, or if he had been totally played. The car pulled up to a stone-faced building that looked like it had been built sometime around the Spanish-American war. A glimmer of hope surfaced as the attitude of the soldiers changed. They opened the door for him and led him into the building. It wasn't quite respect, but neither were there gun-barrels jabbing at him.

A solider held the large, ornate door open for him and followed as they entered the interior, awash with ancient fluorescent lights. Another soldier, clearly holding a higher rank, evident by both his uniform and the deference with which the other men treated him, came forward. Norm thought for a second he was going to shake his hand, but instead he grabbed his bound wrists and forced him forward. Without a word, he was passed off to a more senior man who escorted him down a granite-lined hallway to a closed door he opened with a key from his belt.

Before the door closed, the general entered the room.

"You can't hold me like this," Norm said, trying to establish his position. "You know who I am."

The man spoke as if he had never met him, "This is Cuba." He looked down at him, "We can do whatever we want. I don't think your government will risk an invasion to save you, and after today, relations will be back where they were in the eighties."

He might as well be held in Beijing, he thought, and that might be his eventual destination. The Chinese would be eager for the secrets he held.

***

Mac and Armando were near exhaustion. Forced to tread water, there was nothing to cling to other than the crustacean-covered concrete overhang above them, which would have no mercy on their hands. The sharp mollusks would slice through their skin if they dared to grab hold. He would have liked to hide under the structure, but the jetties were solid underneath, built to support the weight of the buildings, not like most docks supported by piers and girders. Mac searched frantically for a way out, knowing it would be only minutes before the Cubans added boats to their search. The ferry was tied up on the north-facing side of the jetty and they were trapped between the hull of the boat and the structure. Mac could see nothing but steel and concrete. The small sliver of open water at the bow of the boat was the only avenue of escape, but it was too exposed. They would be spotted immediately. Instead he started to swim towards the seawall hoping a yet unforeseen option would present itself. Whatever they did, they had to move - both men were close to failing.

The whine of an outboard engine sounded like it was moving towards them and he swam back under the scant cover of the short overhang. The pursuit was closing in and Mac inhaled deeply, filling his lungs. The only thing he could do until an option presented itself was to avoid the men by going where they weren't. He motioned to Armando that he was about to swim back under the boat. He had no idea how to escape from there, but he had to try.

They swam back under the boat and surfaced on the other side, both men gasping for breath. Mac started to feel chilled, even in the eighty-degree water, and knew they had to get to land. He could hear several boats, but the focus of the search was on the pier side of the ship. Seconds later a man yelled an alarm and a boat approached.

***

Alicia shut down the computers and started to unplug the wires. "Do you have an inverter on the boat?" she asked carrying one of the monitors through TJ's living room and out the door.

"What's she up to?" TJ asked Trufante and turned to the girl. "Yeah, but there's no internet."

"Best just follow along, CIA secret shit and all. You know they'll pay you for this right. They commandeer stuff all the time and pay top dollar," Trufante said.

Alicia smiled allowing his interest and recognition of her computer skills to put a little swagger in her walk. She walked down the steps to the dock, set the monitor down and ran back upstairs for the rest of the equipment. "You guys need to put together some food and water. It's almost two hundred miles." She stared them down. Finally Trufante reached for a twelve pack of beer. "Water," she said and grabbed the router and computer. "This would be easier if you had a laptop."

"Slow down, sister." TJ picked up the monitor and started upstairs. "You just have to ask. I have a fully mobile FOB." TJ went into what she thought was the bedroom, re-emerged and handed her the computer.

"Maybe a tablet too?" she asked hopefully.

"Got one downstairs we use for credit cards and stuff. I suppose you're going to commandeer that too."

She nodded, set down the heavy computer and grabbed the laptop. "Can you guys put a little urgency into this?"

The two men looked at each other and shrugged.

Great, she thought, stuck with a couple of stoners. If her field career hadn't started off badly enough, now she had these two. Finally her stare paid off and the men gathered a cooler of food and several gallons of water. They were about to leave when Trufante grabbed the beer.

"It's a long ride," he said and tucked the box under his arm.

She decided this wasn't a battle worth fighting and looked around the room again. TJ's cell phone was charging on the counter and she grabbed it on her way out. Minutes later they were aboard. Trufante cracked a beer and TJ fired the engine. He called out several orders she didn't understand, something about slipping lines, and they pulled from the dock. She glanced at TJ's phone and took note of the time. It was two o'clock. They needed to be in range by midnight.

"Where's the PFDs?" she asked, already unsteady as the boat left the canal and entered the choppy inshore waters.

TJ shot a look at Trufante who shrugged.

Trufante crossed to her and she flinched. "You can swim, can't you?" he asked

She nodded, wondering what he was getting at. "In a pool, but this is the ocean."

"Water's water. You want to be a secret agent, we gotta break you of some of your fears."

She looked at him, ashamed. "OK. Just tell me where all the safety stuff is."

He gave her a quick tour of the boat, answering her questions, and disappeared up the ladder to the flybridge. She heard two beers open, shook her head in dismay and went into the small cabin.

Minutes later she was set up in the lounge. The laptop sat in front of her, the cell phone next to it. Fully aware the phone would be tracked the minute she enabled it as a hotspot, she worked quickly to download the software she needed to the laptop. She held her breath and clicked the link. Thinking, just another minute and she could turn off the phone, she frantically worked the browser to download the software from the Internet Radio Linking Project. It started slowly and she peered out the windows. If they remained close to land and stayed in the same cell, anyone monitoring the system would not know they were traveling by boat and would assume they were land-based. Once they moved to another cell, they could be tracked.

Finally the software loaded and she disabled the link, shut off the power to the phone and removed the battery. She thought about throwing it overboard, but weighed the risk and decided to keep it. With a click on the trackpad, the install process started and she waited while the timer on the screen flipped back and forth. A confirmation message appeared and she turned to the hand-held VHF radio that Trufante had showed her on his safety tour. She removed the case and examined the ports on the back allowing the unit to be used as a base station. With a knife she had found in the galley, she took the phone charger from TJ's cell phone and cut the cord. With ease, she stripped the wires on the device side, leaving the USB connector. Carefully she inserted the bare wires into the audio out ports on VHF and plugged the connector into the USB port on the computer.

The Echo software started and she held her breath, turned on the VHF radio and set the channel to 79. She had no idea of the network here, but with this many boats, there had to be other enthusiasts who had rigged their radios as repeaters. The screen jumped and she tapped her foot, waiting for a connection. Seconds later, the dual panes on the screen showed a link. She opened the internet browser and typed *Havana map* into the search box. The screen changed and a map slowly became clearer as the image loaded.

The engines came up to speed and she felt vibration change under her feet. She looked away from the screen and out the window again, having to fight a slight wave of nausea as spray shot by the windows, obscuring the comforting view of land. Knowing there was no use in worrying about things she couldn't control, she looked up at the life jackets over her head and reached for one. Ensconced within the comfort of the orange fabric, she watched the video stream of the ferry docking in Havana. That was the good news; a stream of Spanish came over the computer's speakers and she heard the word: *fugitivo*.

TWENTY FIVE

The two men froze when they saw a soldier point straight at them from the bow of an approaching boat. Mac was past fatigue and his body felt heavier with each breath as he fought to keep his head above water. He looked over at Armando who looked like he only had seconds left and Mac worried his decisions could end badly again. Thoughts of surrender crossed his mind and he was about to give up and call to the closest boat when something pulled his leg. His first reaction was to pull back, thinking it was a shark, but he could feel the synthetic material of a glove and was able to grab a deep breath before he felt the cool water embrace him.

The men were pulled to the bottom. A dive mask appeared in his face and a hose with a mouthpiece was handed to him. The diver patiently showed him how the rebreather worked and Mac was soon piggybacked on him, alternating breaths with the awkward hose. The first few tries, he panicked as no air came out, but remembered that unlike an open circuit system where the air was released on demand, the regulator had a manual shutoff to prevent air from escaping. The equipment was designed to recycle and scrub a divers' air, using a succession of filters to remove the CO_2 and add oxygen or mixed gas so that the diver could breathe under water without releasing bubbles. Mac had never used a rebreather, but knew the theory, and his years of diving training and experience paid dividends as he knew he could trust the system. To his right he saw another diver wrestling with Armando.

He tried to attract Armando's attention, hoping he would copy him, but the Cuban was flailing in the water, fighting the diver. Mac knew what had to happen before it did, and was not surprised when the other diver removed his knife and smacked the man several times on the temple with the blunt end. Rescue divers were often injured and sometimes killed by out-of-control victims.

Mac passed the regulator back and forth with the diver below him, the short hose hard to handle, but they soon found a natural rhythm. Armando was calm now, or maybe unconscious and the other diver stood him on the sandy bottom, inserted the mouthpiece in his mouth and opened the air valve. Mac squinted through the murky water, his eyes burning from the salt, but he thought he saw Armando move, and tapped the diver below him, motioning him closer to the two men. They reached them and Mac saw that Armando was conscious, a small stream of green running from his temple. He tapped him and saw the man's eyes open. Once he had his attention he exaggerated the movements to buddy breath with the equipment. Finally, the panic left Armando's face and he calmed down. Both men climbed on the back of the divers, who inflated their buoyancy compensators to stay neutral in the water and started to swim.

Used to the constant stream of bubbles from standard SCUBA gear, the rebreathers were incredibly quiet and it took him a few minutes to adjust to the feeling. The sound of propellers came from above and between breaths he looked up at the surface, barely visible through the harbor water. Through squinted eyes he estimated the visibility was less than ten feet, the other pair barely visible beside him, the ferry lost in the murky water.

They stayed at this level in the eerily dark water, in a kind of purgatory, neither the surface nor the bottom visible. The diver checked his compass and gauges, making small adjustments to their buoyancy and course. Mac kept his eyes shut and focused on his breath, trying to make it easy for the diver below him. His thoughts started to focus as he got more comfortable in the strange surroundings and started speculating where these divers had come from and how they happened to be in a position to save them. There was no way, from the distance they had already travelled, that they had been in the water just to rescue them. No, they had been there doing something else, and Mac thought back to the bomb threat. There was no other explanation and he started to speculate whether they were friend or foe. He felt the diver add air to his BC and ascend. Before he could react, a hand grabbed him from above and he was hoisted from the water.

***

Alicia looked up, wondering what the loud noise was, and smacked her head against TJ who was looking over her shoulder. Instinctively she closed the screen and stared at him, not knowing how long he had been there or what he had seen.

"What is that noise? I'm trying to work here."

He handed her a piece of paper. "Compressor - Just filling the tanks."

"Why now, and what's this?" She pushed the paper aside.

"You said I would be compensated for this. It's a bill," TJ said.

A wave smashed the hull causing the boat to pitch. "Shouldn't you be driving?" she asked and grabbed the table with both hands.

"No worries. Tru's just taking a bit to get used to the joystick. It's all about fine tuning the motor skills. Lot of skill transfer from driving a ten ton boat to a game controller. Now could you help me with this?" He pushed the paper back towards her.

She looked at the sloppy handwriting and figures laid out in an uneven column, thinking the best way to get rid of him was to cooperate. Then she could get back to work. There had been some broken chatter on the VHF she had just picked up in Spanish about men in the water, but there was no way to pinpoint where the signal came from. She adjusted the squelch, but they were too far away to receive a clear signal. Frustrated she looked back at the paper. "What's all this? Provisioning, air fills?" she asked as she scanned the charges.

"Got a charter in the morning; can't fill the tanks at the shop. Heck, I'm, not sure we'll even make it back," he said and grabbed the list from her adding 'missed charter' to the charges.

She took it back and continued reading, "This is crazy. Fifty dollars for a twelve pack of beer that I'm not even drinking."

"It's all supply and demand - gotta keep the crew happy. Besides, Tru said to add everything."

She was getting angry, but also knew the Agency would pay whatever she submitted without question. Other bills, thinly veiled charges for cocaine and hookers, had passed her desk and the Agency paid them without comment. She took the bill back.

"Can you stop the noise?"

He went out to the deck, came back a minute later after shutting off the compressor, the dull rumble of the main engine and the sound of the seas slapping against the hull the only noise. Scary as that had been an hour ago, it was almost calming without the compressor.

"Happy?" he asked.

She ignored him, hoping he would go away, but he remained.

"Anything else?"

"Well, I couldn't help but notice you were scanning the VHF."

She looked up impatiently, waiting for him to continue.

"I worked out an algorithm to triangulate the signals and generate a GPS waypoint for the source of the communication. It's all about getting good numbers in my business. Divers now want more than the *tourista* dives in the books. With this, I see one of my competitors out on a spot and I hit this button," he reached over her. "And shazaam. There you go."

That was the missing piece she had been working on. She slid over and motioned for him to share the bench seat. Just as he sat, another wave threw them together.

"What the ..."

"No problem." He got up. "I'll put the auto-pilot on. Could be that we just entered the stream."

"The what?"

"The Gulf Stream. You know, the current of water that runs from here to Greenland. It can be a bugger sometimes." He got up just as another wave slammed against the boat. "Yup, feels like the stream to me."

She stared out the window. From her vantage point, the top of the waves were at eye level as she looked out the window, looking like they would roll the boat over. A quick tug confirmed the life vest was securely in place and she went back to work. The boat seemed to change course and the seas evened out. She was able to resume work.

TJ came back down to the cabin. "Changed the heading. Should be a bit smoother now."

"Is he still awake up there?" She could feel the last few days catching up to her.

"As long as there's beer, he'll be awake. When we run out is when you have to keep an eye on him."

Not the answer she wanted, she turned the VHF louder and scanned the screen. "This is the signal. Let's see what your program can do." She slid the laptop towards him and watched as he put his head down and started typing. She could usually tell how good a programmer was by their body language, and from watching TJ's focus, she knew he was very good. What a waste to dedicate it to gaming, she thought. A minute later he pushed the screen back to her, a satellite image open with a red dot near three piers.

"Terminal Sierra Maestra," she read the small type. "That's the ferry pier. Something's gone wrong."

She started typing and scanning the screen, oblivious to the eyes looking over her shoulder.

"That's slicker than owl shit," he said.

She needed his cooperation, and if trading off computer tips would garner it, so be it, she thought, and continued to let him read, talking through what she was seeing as the text flew by. "Getting two signals overlapping. One is a search effort for two men that jumped from the ferry, the other is an escort calling ahead that they have two high-ranking Americans in custody and are bringing them in for questioning."

She listened to the chatter, processing the pieces as she listened to the radio and watched the screen. This was her wheelhouse and she relaxed, letting her subconscious work, knowing that it would soon spit out the answers.

"I'm going to need a plan pretty soon. We're past Key West and should be near Cuban waters in a couple of hours."

***

Norm sat in the chair waiting for his captors to return and reveal his fate. There were only three outcomes and only one of those was good: a Cuban jail, death, or release. He expected the latter. A CIA operative at his level had things to offer, either information or a trade. He had probably been missed by now, but with the nature of the business it would be days, or even weeks, before anyone bothered to look for him. Only Alicia had any idea what he was up to and she was also deeply embroiled in this mess. He could only hope that she wouldn't panic. By now he expected her to have tracked him down with her computer skills.

The door opened and the general entered. "We meet again, Mr. CIA," he said.

142

Norm stared at the pock-marked face and waited.

"My grandson is missing. He jumped into the harbor with your accomplice."

Norm suspected something was wrong when he saw Choy walk into the room. "I got him to Cuba. You can find him," he said more bravely than he felt.

"The deal was to hand him over and I would give you the location and time of the bomb." He leaned over, his face close. "You have failed and now you can watch the ferry blow up and everything you have worked for vanish."

"There will be an investigation," Norm stuttered.

"In Cuban waters?" Choy waved his hands in dismissal, "They can say what they want. Relations between the countries will be ruined, maybe permanently, but at least long enough for China to strengthen its foothold here."

"The US will never allow that," Norm said.

"Allow what," Chow spat. "Trade? We have learned to use your own convictions against you. There is no need to start a war when your real weakness is yourselves. The liberal media in your country will be jumping over each other every time a freighter enters Cuban water bearing Chinese goods to improve the lives of the poor Cubans. Make no mistake. We will own this country."

"And what about me?" Norm asked.

TWENTY SIX

He was hauled onto the steel deck and bound. From the quick glimpse he got before they blindfolded him he determined that it was a Navy ship and Cuban from the Spanish being spoken around him. He felt Armando's body next to his as orders were given and they were hauled across the hard deck. The bulkhead slammed into his back as they were dragged inside a cabin and he was alone.

The sound of a helicopter landing startled him and he realized he had lost track of time and thought he might have fallen asleep. The rotors shut down and the ship was quiet again. Although he was in the dark cabin, he could sense men were moving quickly around the boat, and he figured from the changed attitudes that whoever had just landed had something to do with their urgency and his fate. He started to get fidgety. The restraints cut into his wrists with each movement and he was at the point of breaking when the blindfold was ripped from his head. A pock-marked face stared at him.

"You are?" the man asked.

Mac looked at the scarred face, the army uniform displaying enough hardware to suggest his rank. There was no reason to lie to the man. "Mac Travis," he said.

"Ah, Mac Travis. And how did you come to be in the water?"

Mac needed to stall and see where this man's loyalties were. He had figured out enough in the last few days to understand the two factions vying for power. Their means were the same, but their aims were different. "Where is my friend?"

The man laughed, "Your friend? Is that what he is. We know Armando Cruz, the baseball player and my grandson."

"Is he OK?"

"Mac Travis, yes; he is safe and comfortable and thank you for taking care of him, although dragging him into the harbor with you served no purpose. He speaks highly of you and requested that you not be hurt."

His suspicions were confirmed and Mac tried to figure a way out. "What do you intend to do with me then?"

The man rubbed his chin. "You are also a prize," he turned, giving an order in Spanish to one of the men behind him.

***

Alicia was frantically typing lines of code, alternately pinging Mac and Norm's phones. Neither responded and she suspected the batteries were removed or totally dead. Since the men had been captured, the chatter on the radio had become more organized and less urgent. Hoping this meant that they haven't been found yet, she continued working.

She had been fighting her conscience as well. The 'do the right thing' part of her brain told her to call this in to the Agency, but the 'it's your first assignment – don't screw it up' part convinced her to wait a little longer. Her sympathetic qualities were intentionally dimmed to make herself analytical, but in this case she was right and taking emotion out of the situation was the best course. She decided that informing the Agency was not going to diffuse a bomb planted on the ferry; it would only muddy the water, especially with Norm missing. Although her trust for him was gone, she still recognized and respected his skill. She was well aware of the assets the Agency had in the area, and knew they were scarce, and none on the island itself. She was the closest and most aware of the situation. Her mother had said to be careful what you wish for, and this was the perfect example.

Frustrated with her efforts, she left the table and made her way to the flybridge. Trufante and TJ sat side by side on the bench, drinking beer like they were out for a pleasure cruise. She climbed the stainless steel ladder and found it was even rougher on the platform, the little bit of elevation making a huge difference in the sway of the boat. With both hands clinging to the rail, she looked ahead. The view was better than the cabin window and she could see the thin line of land ahead.

145

"Is that Cuba?" she asked.

TJ turned to her. "It is. Time to decide; we're sitting just outside their waters."

***

Choy had not shown any willingness to negotiate earlier and Norm paced the room trying to figure a way out. He had picked at the plate of picadillo that sat on the table, pulling the peas out before eating, and wishing the bottled water was rum. He knew the general was trying to appear to be patient, but he suspected he was anxious for a resolution. Having lost control over Choy's grandson, though, things were different. The door opened and the general entered.

"It seems my grandson has been found," he said with a smile.

"Then I am done here. Tell me where the bomb is and let's end this before it turns into an international incident."

"Not so fast, Mr. CIA. Maybe we should take a walk," Choy said and extended his arm toward the door.

Norm didn't have to be asked twice. 'Take a walk' in the intel business meant the general wanted to talk without anyone hearing. He had to suspect, or know firsthand, that the building was monitored. Norm walked out the door and past the guard, the general behind him. They exited the building from a back door and entered a small park-like area surrounded by a high concrete wall.

The general started to walk and as they reached the far corner of the property, he stopped. "I can trust your discretion?"

Norm knew what this meant as well; he was about to be asked an off-the-books favor. "Of course," he replied.

"We don't need to go into the inner politics of the island. I trust you know what is going on here," Choy said.

"Yes," Norm said, showing more patience than he felt.

"But things are not often as they appear." He started walking. "I am an old man. You see, I came here with my countrymen over fifty years ago, full of dogma, a desire to support the revolution, and thwart the evil United States. Over the years I have become more and more Cuban and less Chinese. I intermarried, out of necessity, and raised my children and grandchildren under the name Cruz, rather than Choy."

Norm knew where this was going.

Choy continued. "The younger generations of my family have blended and assimilated well, to the point where my grandson is a well known Cuban baseball player. But you already know that." He paused and looked at the ground. "I have seen three brands of communism fail, all in different fashions: the Russians first, with their power-hungry greed; my home country with their nepotism and hatred of the peasants; and my adopted country. I care for these people and call them my own."

He stopped and looked at Norm. "I am powerless in this. The Special Forces men that captured your Mac Travis and rescued my grandson were there to plant the bomb on the ferry. I have no reason to believe they did not succeed."

Norm saw the opening. "And how can I help you, General?"

"I am going to release you. Since there is no US embassy here, you are on your own."

"You want me to find and diffuse the bomb?" He needed an answer to a question that had been bothering him now that he held the higher ground. "So this was always a bluff."

The look on the general's face said it all.

"Where are you holding the American?" Norm asked, playing his advantage. He needed to find Travis and close the loop on this.

"Fair enough. I don't want any more blood on my hands," Choy said.

***

Mac felt someone grab him by the shirt, pull him to his feet and push him towards a passageway. He was guided along the narrow corridor and stopped at a cabin close to what he thought, by the increasing engine noise, was the stern. The man pushed him. He tripped on a threshold and was thrown against a steel wall. Something slammed behind him and his hopes sunk another notch when he heard the sound of the hatch being sealed. It took a few minutes for his eyes to acclimate to the dimly lit cabin. It was a plain storage closet barely big enough for him to move. The walls were lined with shelves containing what looked like cleaning supplies, some with Russian labels.

He sat down and leaned against the steel bulkhead, trying to figure out a plan, but soon realized how futile his situation was. Stuck in the hold of a foreign Navy ship somewhere in Cuba was not anywhere close to a scenario he could salvage, and he started to feel powerless to help Mel.

His leg cramped, probably from dehydration, and he twisted to the side to relieve the pain. He heard the sound of something hit the steel deck and worked his hand around to find the objet that must have fallen from his pocket. He thought back to his capture or rescue, not sure if he needed to make the distinction, and could not recall being searched. Dragged dripping wet from the water in only shorts and a T-shirt, it was evident he was weaponless. His hand found the plastic case of the cell phone and he groaned. After being in the water, there was little chance it would work.

He flipped the screen open and nothing happened, although that didn't surprise him. With nothing else to do, he crawled to the door and searched the bulkhead for a light. His hand found a toggle switch that turned on a single overhead bulb in a metal cage and he surveyed his surroundings. The shelves were lined with cleaning supplies and paper goods. He looked down at the dead phone and cleared a workspace on a shelf, pulled the cover off the back compartment and removed the battery. With a roll of toilet paper, he wiped the terminals clean and placed it to the side. Slowly he scanned the supplies stored on the shelves until he found what looked like glass cleaner. He squirted a small amount on his finger, smelled it and felt it evaporate.

There were no ingredients listed on the generic looking products, but he suspected the cleaner contained a high volume of isopropyl alcohol. He took the bottle back to the shelf and pried the phone case apart. The toilet paper had a harsh industrial feel to it and though he wouldn't want to use it for its intended purpose, it was better than its softer counterpart for his use. Working carefully he dried the board inside the phone by dabbing it with a wad of the paper. When he had gotten all the moisture the paper could reach, he picked up the cleaner and sprayed down the phone. It seemed incongruent to his purpose, but he knew rubbing alcohol was a drying agent and would leach the remaining moisture from the circuit board when it evaporated. The unknown was time. There was no telling what other ingredients were in the solution and they would all dry at different rates. It looked dry so he replaced the battery and turned the unit on. It was either going to work or not and he might as well find out now.

He pressed the power button, but heard activity in the hallway and quickly pushed back his work, set several boxes in front of it and lunged for the light switch. The door opened and he assumed the position on the floor.

Squinting at the light, he tried to make it appear to his captors that he had been in the dark the whole time. He clenched his jaw when one of the men started sniffing the chemicals still in the air, but the soldier moved out of the way when the pock-faced man came towards him and slammed his head with a leather sap.

TWENTY SEVEN

"I got a signal!" Alicia called up to the flybridge. She went back into the cabin and started typing. The further they had traveled from the US coast, the fewer and further apart the repeaters were. Reception was poor, but she had just gotten a notification that Mac's phone had just turned on and she raced to pinpoint the location before she lost the signal.

TJ hovered over her as she worked. "Can we call him?"

"If I had more time, I could hack into the Cuban cell network, but it's notoriously unreliable. Here is the position." She handed him a piece of paper with the GPS coordinates.

"We can plug them in the unit on the bridge," he said and shot out of the cabin.

Before she followed, she tried Norm's phone again, but the screen remained blank. She left the cabin, glanced at the seas, gripped the narrow stainless steel ladder tightly and followed TJ to the bridge. Both men had their heads together entering the numbers in the chart plotter. He looked up at Alicia and pointed to the dot on the screen.

"In the middle of Havana Harbor." He said the words as if the name held some evil menace.

"We have to assume he's in trouble. There would be no other reason for him to be there," she said, trying to figure out a scenario that explained his position on what must be a ship. "Why there?"

"We gotta save him," Trufante said.

Alicia looked at the dot on the screen. She could feel her heart beat in her chest as she stared at the electronic connection like a frail umbilical cord. She knew policy and the danger of entering Cuban waters, but there was the bomb, and that should have been enough, with the lives of hundreds of people at stake. She also felt she owed something to Mac after he had saved her from the meth heads in the backwaters of Florida Bay.

"I have to go research international maritime law," she said and started to walk away.

"The law ain't going to save him," Trufante said.

She knew he was right, but procedure was her crutch. There had to be another way. "I have an idea. How far are we from Cuban waters?"

"The line's right there." Trufante traced his finger on the screen. "Twelve miles offshore."

An idea was blooming in her head. "TJ, have you heard about the Cuban government giving permission to US-based dive charters to enter their waters?" They had the perfect cover with the dive boat.

"Sure. I know a few guys running six-pack trips, overnighters from Key West."

She could see the concern in his face when he realized what she was up to. "Let's go," she told Trufante, who wasted no time in changing course.

"Wait!" TJ pushed Trufante's hand from the joystick and twisted it back towards Florida. "You can't take my boat in there. They'll blow us out of the water."

"Do we have to go through this again?" she asked in her most authoritative voice.

"Damn, buddy, this shit'll make you famous. Them gamers you chat up won't believe it." Trufante turned the wheel to the south. "Best listen to the lady."

TJ stood back, a deep frown on his face.

"This is not just about Mac; there are hundreds of lives at stake, never mind the political fallout if that bomb goes off." She hoped to guilt him into submission with the moral obligation argument. She could see him thinking. "And, I can show you a back door to dominate World of Warcraft."

His expression changed and she knew they had won him over.

"Anything happens to the boat, the CIA takes care of it - right?"

"Add it to your bill," she said, gaining confidence. "Now here's our story when they question us."

***

"Get up, Mr. Travis."

Mac felt a hand tug at him and slowly opened his eyes. A man stood over him. He grimaced, put his hand to the lump on his head and rubbed it as if that would make the headache go away. His hand came back free of blood. He stared at the man.

"You have a visitor," the pockmarked man said, signaling one of the soldiers to escort him from the storeroom.

Mac followed him onto the deck. It was night; how late he didn't know. He tried to find the moon but was blinded by the ship's lights. The only thing past the deck of the boat he could see was the twinkling from the shore and the white anchor lights from several boats. He followed the man to an open section of rail on the starboard side. They stood there watching the red and green bow lights of a fast boat approach. Mac struggled to see who was aboard. Fenders were tossed and it coasted to a stop against the steel hull, received the lines tossed to them by a crew member and tied off. A ladder was dropped from the deck and a man climbed aboard.

They stood facing each other, neither speaking until Norm motioned the soldiers away.

"Well, Travis, seems you're in a bit of trouble here."

Mac just stared at him, both thankful he had arrived and knowing he couldn't trust him.

"They have Armando. I did what you asked," Mac started.

"I know, and you want your girlfriend brought back from the dead, and your life and boat back. It sounds like a broken record," Norm said and leaned on the rail. "Do I have to remind you there are only a handful of people that know you are alive."

They both looked over the rust-stained rail at the lights of Havana. Mac saw what he thought was the ferry terminal. The ferry appeared to be where it had docked earlier in the day. He breathed in the humid night air and listened to the sounds of Havana brought into the harbor by the light breeze blowing in his face. There had to be a reason Norm had appeared and he didn't expect it was to take him home and make everything better.

152

"You might be wondering what is next for you?" Norm asked.

Mac took his time; the only negotiation tactic he had ever mastered was silence. "Yes," he finally answered. The CIA man seemed to be relishing the drama.

"At daybreak you will dive with the team that rescued you. They are training on this dive site we are anchored on, ironically the 'USS Maine'. Do you know your history?"

Mac nodded, but Norm felt the need to talk.

"In 1898 she exploded right on this spot taking two-hundred-and-sixty men to the bottom of the harbor. It was the inciting incident that triggered the Spanish-American war."

"They floated the ship and towed it to sea," Mac said, wondering where this was going.

"So you are paying attention. Correct, but there are still armaments down there." He looked at the dark water. "They built a cofferdam around what was left of the ship, floated and towed it to sea back in the early 1900's. There have been several inquiries, but the Castro's have had no interest."

Mac was starting to put the pieces together.

Norm continued. "Now that relations have improved, the government has authorized this training mission to find any personal effects or remains of the crew that they can pass to the families."

"And under the cover of a relations building training mission, several men found live munitions which they have rigged the ferry with. That explains why the divers were on rebreathers and under the boat when we went in."

"Very good, Travis."

"So why don't you bring in a demolitions team to diffuse the bomb?" Mac asked, but knew the answer before the words were out of his mouth.

"I have." Norm stared at him.

***

Alicia stared at the screen showing the radar signatures of the ships from Palm Beach to St. Thomas. The Automatic Identification System required most vessels in international waters to have a transponder aboard, but apparently the Cuban government had not gotten that memo. The shipping lanes were crowded with icons representing the tankers, freighters and pleasure boaters, except for the large blank space around Cuba. She was looking for any threat, but TJ's boat rarely ventured further than the reef, only five miles from Key Largo, and had no need for radar. The AIS system was no help here.

TJ had told her they were anchored on a reef in forty feet of water off the coast of Havana, just out of sight of the Castillo and the harbor entrance. She rubbed her eyes and decided to take a break. Needing some fresh air, she went on deck. The seas were close to flat and she felt strangely at ease standing in the same spot that had terrified her earlier. The moonlight promised good fishing to the handful of boats roaming the reef, and to an onlooker from shore they would look like any other boat. She looked back over the transom at the shore line and couldn't help but notice the lack of light, at least compared to Miami. The darkness was interrupted occasionally by a car cruising the coastal road. Otherwise this part of the coast was barren. TJ had chosen well.

The two men had run out of beer before dark and she could hear Trufante snoring in the forward berth. TJ was on the flybridge keeping watch. Mac's request to check on Mel nagged at her and she went back inside and sat down at her make-shift work station. The chatter on the radio had died and with no new information coming in, she minimized the window.

Hacking into the server was child's play, except for the dial-up-like speed from the two repeaters she was able to connect to, but she was soon combing through the admitted patients records. She scrolled through the names, realizing that he had never called her anything except Mel. Melanie Woodson was the closest match and she clicked on her file. The entries were chronological, from her admittance earlier in the week until the latest, one only an hour ago. She was trained to notice inconsistencies in data and her eyes focused on an entry made earlier that day. The doctor's name was unique and she clicked on the entry. As she read it, a tear formed in her eye. The entry described the test results, with a conclusive statement at the end that the patient was, in the doctor's opinion, brain dead. With no training, the tests were meaningless, but her curiosity was not satisfied. She copied and pasted the doctor's name into a search engine and waited for the results.

It wasn't hard to find what she was looking for with a name like Dr. Moran Kowalski, and the page quickly populated. The first entries were basic info, but farther down the page were a series of articles from several

Virginia newspapers about an inquiry into the doctor. She pulled up the first one, started reading, and held her breath when she saw the firm of Davies and Associates represented him. Further down, the article stated the all too similar case history. The doctor had been brought in to evaluate a patient and declared him brain dead without first ruling out the list of criteria that prevented the diagnosis. The patient had come out of his coma and the family sued. The next appearance of Moran Kowlaski was in Miami a year later.

She noticed the waning battery, dashed off an email to an associate who she hoped would look into the matter, and closed the cover. Exhausted, she leaned against the corner of the settee and closed her eyes.

TWENTY EIGHT

Mac felt like he was somewhere in the death march of a prisoner about to be executed, but was unsure how far off the end was. He had been woken before dawn, fed a bland breakfast, and led to the dive briefing room on the ship. Equipment was laid out on the deck in front of benches where a half-dozen men were checking their gear and talking quietly. He was directed to an empty section of the bench and started to fumble with the rebreather pack, watching the other divers as he copied their movements.

His first experience with this type of equipment, made to increase bottom time by recycling the air expelled by the diver through scrubbers and enrichers, had been buddy-breathing only yesterday. The equipment was in pieces. He tried to follow along with the diver next to him and assemble his. Everything connected, he checked the regulator, panicking that he had done something wrong when no air flowed. The diver next to him tapped the knob on the mouthpiece and he remembered having to turn on and off the air manually.

He looked at the diver and pointed to the depth gauge, wondering how deep they were going to dive to judge the particular air mixture in the pack. Although he was not experienced with the equipment, he had been diving with mixed gasses since their introduction. The additional bottom time, lack of decompression issues and the better mental state at depth made it indispensable in all the time he had spent in the water.

The diver said something in Spanish, but Mac couldn't count past ten and shrugged his shoulders. The man picked up the gauge and pointed to the fifteen foot line. Mac gave him a questioning look, but the diver pointed to the line again. He had not been able to see top to bottom when he was in the water the other day, but he could tell by the pressure changes in his ears that it was deeper.

Confused was no way to start a dive in murky, unfamiliar waters and he wondered what other problems he would have with the equipment. He picked up the booties left for him, looked at the European size and realized what the confusion with the depth gauge had been. Everything was in metric. He picked up the gauge again and realized it was in meters.

With that knowledge he checked the gear again, studying the gauges that would monitor his system. If he got it wrong, he could easily die. Satisfied for now, he knew he would have to second guess every decision he made while in the water, but at least he knew from the other diver that the maximum depth would be forty-five feet. Even with standard air and equipment, that would allow over an hour of bottom time.

An officer entered the room and the men stopped talking and directed their attention to him. He started speaking in Spanish, using a white-board with a diagram of what looked like the skeletal remains of the Maine drawn on it, its parts scattered across a vast area. He called out names and he drew stick figures on the board, telling each diver where they were expected to work. When he'd finished, he came over to Mac.

"That equipment is not for you."

Mac looked up at the man, not wanting to give him any excuse to pull him from the dive. This could be his only chance for escape.

"We have a diver out. I have standard gear." He went to a storage locker and pulled out the more familiar BC and regulator.

Mac accepted the gear and inspected it. The depth gauge read in feet and the pressure gauge in pounds per square inch, the units he was familiar with. His confidence rose when the man hauled a steel cylinder labelled nitrox out of the locker and set it on the deck. The gear eased his mind slightly, but he still had the problem of the bomb and his escape. He was about to ask for the rebreather, which would eliminate his bubbles, making him virtually invisible in the harbor water, but decided he had a better chance with the standard gear.

"What is the mixture?" he asked. Nitrox was a broad term for mixed gasses and in order for him to know his limits, the information was critical. Ideally he would have liked to verify the mix, but under these conditions he would have to trust the man.

"It is a thirty-six percent mix."

Mac nodded at the familiar blend. The atmospheric air contained twenty-one percent oxygen; the enriched blend increased the oxygen levels and reduced the nitrogen. He ran the numbers in his head. At forty-five feet he would run out of air before he ran out of bottom time.

Norm had explained the scenario last night and it all worked until the end. His cover was that of an observer sent by the United States to oversee the work on the 'Maine'. He was then to slip off and remove the munition placed on the propeller shaft of the ferry and return. Norm had promised him he would be a free man if he succeeded, but he had no confidence in that and saw this as his only chance to escape. He assembled the gear and suited up, carefully checking the straps and buckles on the BC. He swept his right arm around his side to retrieve the regulator, set it in his mouth and breathed in. One last check of the gauges and he was ready.

A red light came on by the door and the divers stood and shuffled single-file towards the hatch. Mac followed the group and heard the sound of water being pumped out of a compartment. The light turned green and the divers followed the lead man, who opened the hatch and entered the chamber. When all the men were inside, the door was closed and locked behind them. It began to fill with water. The men made final adjustments to their equipment and waited for the compartment to flood.

Mac waited until the water reached his neck before inserting the regulator in his mouth. Seawater reached the ceiling and the lead man opened the hatch, causing a slight bump as the pressures equalized. One by one, the men started to swim away from the boat.

They swam as a group towards the bow of the ship, reached the anchor line and followed it towards the bottom. Visibility was better than yesterday, probably the influence of the clear water brought with the incoming tide, but it was still murky, more like the polluted waters of Galveston where he had been trained, than the clear water of the Keys. As they descended, the bottom came into view and he cleared his ears to balance the increasing pressure in his head. The divers fanned out over the area, each going to his assigned position. Remnants of the cofferdam that had been used to float the ship were still visible, the area inside mostly void of wreckage, but as the divers moved into their positions outside of the wreck area, the flotsam became more common. Mac, although naturally intrigued, checked his compass and moved slowly in the direction of the ferry.

There was no way to tell if he was being followed as the water closed around him, and he guessed that even if he was being watched, it would appear the sea had swallowed him. The wreck was invisible when he looked back. He checked his course again and finned harder towards the ferry, writing his headache off to the blow by the general and the pressure from the depth of the dive, breathing slowly to conserve as much air as possible.

***

The wind had picked up and that comfortable feeling Alicia had felt the night before was gone. The orange life preservers were the first thing she saw when she opened her eyes and she wondered if it was a sign. She sat up and put her feet on the deck, slowly getting used to the motion of the boat before standing and moving towards the head.

TJ and Trufante were on the bridge already, eating chips and staring at the small whitecaps the wind had brought.

"Looking a little nautical today, Chi-fon," Trufante said.

"Nice breakfast, boys," she said, hoping the provisions on the bill that TJ had given her were more to her liking, or at least palatable. "Anything on the radar or chatter on the VHF?" she asked.

"All clear," TJ said.

She carefully climbed down the ladder and went back inside the cabin. As she sat in front of the computer, she could feel the nausea rise in her stomach. After quickly scanning the chatter from the last few hours, she grabbed a life jacket and made it outside to the deck just in time to lose the contents of her stomach over the side. She heard the two men laughing on the bridge, hoped it was not at her expense, and staggered back to the protection of the cabin.

After draining half a bottle of water that did nothing for the taste in her mouth, she sat back on the settee and tightened the life jacket. She opened the cover of the laptop and powered the unit up. It took a few minutes to tune the VHF to the lone repeater unit in the area. She connected to the CIA portal and scanned through the chat from the night before. Nothing of interest caught her attention and she opened another program and waited for it to acquire the cell frequency from Mac's phone. An hourglass flipped up and down on the screen, reminding her of the feeling in her stomach. She tried to concentrate, but after a few minutes, the screen showed nothing. She fought through the seasickness and typed some code, trying to troubleshoot the program, but there was no response. The battery in the phone was either totally dead or the device was destroyed.

With the bomb still unaccounted for, she opened a browser and Googled the ferry schedule. Again the hourglass appeared and she had to wait for the page to load. With only the one distant repeater, she became frustrated with the primitive service. Finally the page loaded and she scanned the schedule. The ferry was to depart at nine am. She leaned back, frustrated and sick, wondering what she could do in the hour that remained. Fighting off the growing nausea, she closed her eyes and tried to concentrate. The only thing left was to figure out where the most likely place to detonate the bomb would be and plan accordingly.

The goal of the Chinese Cubans responsible for the plot was to stall or destroy the new relations with the United States. In order to do that, they had to portray themselves as heroes and the Americans as villains. There was nothing to be gained by detonating the bomb in the deep water of the Straights, where it would take weeks to stage an investigation as to the cause of the sinking. The water was too deep and there would be no witnesses. She ruled out Key West, as it would look like an off-the-shelf terrorist plot to blow the ferry, and concentrated on the harbor.

An explosion inside the harbor would be witnessed by thousands and allow the Cubans the chance to mount an immediate rescue operation that would be carried by every media outlet in the world. They would also control any investigation. It would be easy to point fingers at the United States, where factions, many of them Cuban, disagreed with the administration's olive branch approach. They felt the new relationship, and the money it brought with it, would only strengthen the existing government, not unseat them. The groups insisted on the removal of the Castros from power and a democratic government as the only acceptable outcome. Nothing short of another revolution would satisfy them and the Chinese would be closer to their goal of controlling the island.

She closed the laptop and slid out of the settee, bracing herself against the bulkhead, she made her way onto the deck and climbed the ladder to the bridge.

"We have to go into the harbor," she said to the two men. "That's where they are going to blow the ferry."

"What about Mac?" Trufante asked.

"I can't get a signal, but we have to assume he is in trouble." A thought entered her mind. What the Chinese needed was an American scapegoat, and if they had Mac in custody, they could use him.

TWENTY NINE

Norm gripped the rail tightly as the Zodiac skimmed over the chop and approached the pier. He looked into the water for the bubble trail that would mark Travis' location, but the dark water yielded nothing. The plan was in motion and he felt the familiar knot in his stomach. He was powerless. The colonel in charge of the divers had assured him the gas mixture was right and that Travis should be floating to the surface any second. Crowds were already forming on the docks and he checked his watch. The ferry was scheduled to leave soon and there was no sign of Travis. The Zodiac dodged several other small boats also combing the water for the body of the traitor, who would be held up for ridicule by both countries for his attempt to sabotage the ferry. Norm would be a hero for uncovering the plot and Choy would have a lever to slow the development of the two countries' blossoming relationship.

He looked up at the pier, bustling with activity in preparation for the return trip to Key West. People were lined up, waiting to enter the terminal, impatient to get on board. There were two lines; one short for the Americans returning, the other longer for Cubans nervously waiting to clear the exhaustive process of paperwork and inquisition before they were allowed to leave the country. Several media trucks were onsite, their raised antennae visible over the throngs. A large police presence was visible, forcing any onlookers without a ticket away from the pier.

The boats prowling the harbor only added to the feeling of security and didn't look out of place to the Cubans, used to an armed presence in their lives. The Zodiac pulled alongside the empty edge of the pier where two soldiers waited, lines in hand, to help secure it. Just as one of the soldiers reached down to help him out, an alarm was raised from another boat.

"*Vamanos,*" he yelled to the sailor at the helm. He had to see first-hand what the alarm was. The sailor looked confused, but Norm stared him down and the man, scared of his authority, called out in Spanish. The men released the lines and the Zodiac floated away from the dock. Norm heard voices yelling from the other side of the pier and pointed to the helmsman, who reversed enough to clear the dock before accelerating towards open water. Two other boats were closing on the far side of the pier and he moved to the bow to get a better vantage point.

The helmsman slowed as they reached the other boats and coasted alongside the ferry. Several men were pointing at a trail of bubbles and he knew Travis was still alive.

***

Mac moved slowly through the water, constantly checking his gauges. He followed the compass course towards the ferry. Visibility was growing worse with each passing minute. The pier came into view and he started to feel a strange kind of tunnel vision he had only experienced at depths over a hundred feet. He tried to shake the feeling from his head, blaming it on poor visibility or the stress and lack of sleep of the past week. With thousands of hours in the water, the only time he had experienced this feeling was when the air was bad. The divers on the ship were using state-of-the-art equipment; surely there would be a proper mixing station on the boat. Whatever the cause, he forced himself to work through the growing discomfort.

The outline of the twin hulls of the ferry was close and he adjusted his buoyancy to hold him at the level of its port keel. He felt better. The symptoms seemed to relent as he ascended. Another check of his depth and air assured him he was still well in the comfort zone. With only twenty feet of water over his head and almost two-thousand PSI of air in his tank, he would have an hour to find the bomb and diffuse it. He had carefully monitored his depth and speed to conserve air to this point, still unsure what he would do after the bomb was dealt with.

Details of the hull were now clearly visible. He let some air out of the BC, dropped ten feet to clear the keel, and started to inspect the freshly painted steel. The bow area was clean and he moved to the mid-ship, where he found and inspected several round openings flush with the hull. None were large enough for a bomb of any size and the petcocks, preventing water from entering the hole, appeared to be closed. As he reached the stern, he saw the propeller on each hull disrupting the smooth lines of the bottom and swam towards them. If there was a logical place to disable a boat, it would be here. He finished his inspection and move to the starboard hull.

Something caught his eye as he closed the gap to the propeller. The low hum of the engines reverberated through the water, forcing him to keep his distance. So long as the boat remained in neutral, he was safe, but once engaged, he would be sucked into the turbulence of the propellers and torn to shreds. The tunnel vision, which he continued to battle, closed his field of vision, but he fought against it and finned towards the steel shaft where he saw a thin wire.

He inflated the BC to pin himself under the hull and worked closer to the propeller, careful to keep his distance in case the transmission was engaged. For now though, the boat was still in neutral, the shaft vibrating harmlessly with the engine. With his vision narrowing and his head pounding, he thought he saw a wire wrapped around the shaft, and he quickly descended below the blades. The wire led him to a large spool on the bottom sitting next to an old munition, probably from the wreckage of the Maine. His brain was not working at full efficiency, but he recognized the device for what it was and swam to the bomb.

Suddenly the water churned and he could feel the wash from the propeller. The boat started to move. The wire was quickly pulled from the spool and he knew he had to disconnect the munition before all the wire was sucked into the propeller; the bomb attached to the end would be ignited on impact. He had no time to think about the ingenuity of the time-delay fuse. The spool spun faster and he had to dodge it as it flew back and forth and wire reeled off it. He could see the wooden center now and panicked. The bomb was seconds away from being sucked into the propeller and detonating but the line suddenly stopped moving. He looked up and saw the propellers idling. With no idea why, he seized the opportunity. The spool was almost empty now and he grabbed the cylinder before it was pulled towards the hull. His fingers grasped the carabiner connecting the bomb to the wire, but with his dexterity hampered by the bad air, he fumbled it. The transmission engaged and the wire started to peel off the spool again. He was dragged through the water towards the spinning blades and guessed the hull was less than fifty feet away when he finally managed to release the clip.

***

Alicia clung to the stainless steel rail as TJ worked the joystick and surfed the boat into the harbor entrance. Trufante stood beside her, every tooth of his Cadillac grin visible, clearly enjoying the ride. They were past the ancient fortifications left by the Spanish and into the main channel. TJ pulled the throttle back when they passed a marker warning him to slow to idle speed.

"What now?" Trufante asked.

She looked around as the channel opened into the large harbor and saw the ferry on the right. "There."

"And what are we doing when we get there. Look!" He pointed. "There's a gang of navy boats patrolling around it. We'll be locked up as soon as they see us."

Before she could answer, several small boats accelerated and closed on the ferry. "There!" She pointed towards the action.

"They'll blow us out of the water the second they see the registration." TJ pointed at the Navy ship anchored in the middle of the harbor.

She scanned the shore, looking for any way to reach the ferry. "That pier there." She pointed at a commercial dock off their starboard side.

"And then what?"

There was only one way to get close enough to see what was going on. She looked down at the deck behind them. "We've got to get in the water. The dock is empty. We can use the tanks and swim over."

"We?" Trufante asked, his grin gone. "Only two of us here that can do that, and we're civilians."

She had one card to play. "What about Mac? It could be him. If not, the ferry is going to blow up and all those people are going to die." She waited while Trufante processed the information. "Please. There is no other way." She stared him down and could see him waver.

"You good if I get wet?" he asked TJ.

"We're already this deep into it. The only chance to get out of here is for you to be a hero."

"Long way to swim," Trufante said.

"There's a scooter in the forward berth. Not sure what kind of charge is on it. That'll get you there."

Alicia stood there, still grasping the rail. The two men climbed down the ladder and TJ started pulling gear out of a deck box. Time seemed to accelerate as she watched the Navy boats close on the ferry. She looked down at the deck. Trufante was geared up. He placed his mask over his face and looked towards the cabin where TJ emerged with the scooter. Trufante put the regulator in his mouth and looked up at her, raised his thumb and flipped backwards over the side. She gasped, thinking something was wrong, but his head popped up a second later and he took the scooter from TJ. A strange feeling encompassed her as he submerged. She realized this was the first time she had ordered someone into harm's way.

TJ climbed back onto the bridge and pulled a pair of binoculars from the console. He studied the water, but whatever he was looking at was invisible to her.

***

Norm saw a head break the surface of the water several boat lengths ahead. The men in the other boats were yelling back and forth, some on radios, trying to figure out what to do. Third world forces were notorious for waiting for orders instead of taking action and Norm used the delay to his advantage. Unlike the inexperienced crewmen, he had years of experience in the field and was able to see the situation clearly. Travis was on the surface, gasping for air, a round cylinder clutched under his arm. Norm looked at the men huddled around the console waiting for orders, then at the shore and saw a crowd forming, media men with cameras pushing their way through for a better view. It didn't take his trained mind long to realize the best outcome. There would be a lot to explain if he was caught on tape watching from the boat as the Navy men either killed or captured Travis. His best bet was to take him himself. In one swift motion, he grabbed a knife from one of the men and dove in the water.

Although he knew his foe was stronger and better in the water, he was counting on the effect of the nitrogen-laden gas Travis had been breathing to have a debilitating effect and he was confident he could take him. Several strokes later, he reached him, grabbed the air hose feeding the regulator and sliced it with the knife. The mayhem caused by the hose whipping around would further confuse Travis and also provide a distraction for what he needed to do. It would also serve to empty the tank, leaving no evidence of the bad air when the incident was investigated.

He saw the recognition in his eyes as Travis fought to keep his head above water. With his arm around Mac's neck, he pushed him down. His next strike punctured the bladder of the BC. It expelled its air in a burst and the two men sank into the silt. Travis dropped the cylinder and tried to fight. Norm increased the pressure around his neck, trying to put a sleeper hold on him, and fought the urge to breathe waiting for the body to go limp. His brain was almost in panic mode, knowing it needed air, when he released the body. He kicked off the silt and fought to reach the surface when something struck him in his side. Barely able to see in the dark water, he panicked, thinking it was a shark, and fought for the surface. A hand reached out and grabbed him. He was pulled down to the bottom and fought the urge to breathe, choking on the foul harbor water as he lost consciousness.

THIRTY

Mac opened his eyes and instinctively swept his right arm to his side to retrieve the regulator. He grabbed the hose and jammed the mouthpiece between his teeth, but there was no air. He spat out the worthless regulator and released the body, ready to use his last reserves to try and reach the surface. He gagged, his lungs empty now and was about to give in when a hand grabbed him and stuck something in his mouth. Fresh air flowed into his lungs and he breathed deeply, thinking he was in another world when he saw the unmistakable grin in front of his face. Trufante took the regulator back and handed him the octopus. His mind started to clear after several breaths and he surveyed the bottom. Trufante was next to him, the inert body of the CIA man floated beside them.

The bomb lay in the silt, already partially covered by the shifting sands. Mac swam for it, dragging Trufante by the air hose, and swept his hand back and forth to reveal its scarred surface. The hundred-year-old casing appeared to be intact, the only sign of the century in the sea were small rust dots, but none looked like they penetrated the thick shell.

Trufante held the gauges up for Mac to see. The air pressure was hovering around a thousand PSI. With both men sharing the tank, they would be out of air in ten minutes. Not sure how far they had to travel, he saw the panicked look on Trufante's face and knew it would be close. There was no time to diffuse the bomb. He wasn't worried, knowing it would take a percussion, like impact with the propeller or a firing pin, to detonate it. They swam towards the scooter and saw Norm's body start to rise. The discovery of the body might divert attention from their escape, but it could also trigger a man-hunt that could seal them in the harbor. Mac motioned to Trufante, grabbed Norm's body and started finning towards the bomb.

The two men lifted the bomb onto the body anchoring it to the seafloor. Mac glanced back to inspect their work and swam to the scooter. Trufante grabbed the handles and pulled the trigger while Mac attached himself to his back, anxious to get out of the area before the body was found. With the divers already on the 'Maine', they could be diverted to the ferry and be scouring the bottom in minutes. The chain of command was slow, but not broken.

Mac judged they were moving at a little over two knots, but with the incoming tide it felt like they were standing still. He started kicking, wondering where the trade-off would be between the additional air required for the exertion, and the extra speed. He decided it was better to risk the air and get away from the site. He kicked harder, urging Trufante to do the same. They were making progress, and with the clean air, he was able to think as he relied on the Cajun to navigate. With Norm dead, there was only Alicia to clear his name. She wasn't much help in the field, but was a whiz with the computer.

Suddenly the scooter started to lose power and he saw the red light for the battery charge. The dead weight of the scooter dragged them to the bottom. Mac was fading fast, the effect of the bad air still working through his system and looked at Trufante. They ditched the machine and swam side by side into the current. Mac reached down to check the gauges and saw the air was below the red line. With less than five-hundred PSI, they would have only minutes to reach their destination. He felt weaker and blacked out for a second before recovering enough to attract Trufante's attention before his eyes closed.

***

"What do you mean you unplugged the charger from the scooter. That's their only way out." TJ stared at the water with the binoculars.

"I didn't know." She was near tears. "I needed the outlet for the computer."

"We can only hope they make it back," TJ said.

Alicia squinted into the sun and watched the scene around the ferry. Boats circled the site and she saw the splash of divers entering the water.

She could only wonder what was going on below.

"Shit," TJ said watching the course of several larger boats.

Alicia didn't need the binoculars to see they were heading to the harbor entrance. In minutes they would be captive. *Come on, come on.* She started an internal chant, willing the men towards the boat, then she saw a hump on the surface of the water several hundred yards away.

"There!" she pointed, getting TJ's attention.

"Saw that: think it's a turtle," he said and moved the binoculars away.

She continued to watch the area. Whatever it was disappeared, but then she thought she saw bubbles moving towards them.

"It's them!" She pointed again.

TJ moved the glasses and focused on the water, "Damn if you're not right." He put the glasses back in the console, worked the joystick and pushed down on the throttle. "Keep pointing. Don't take your eyes off them," he yelled over the engines.

The boat plowed towards the bubble stream and he reduced speed when they were close, hovering a safe distance away to keep the divers clear of the propellers. He set the boat in neutral.

"We need to signal them," Alicia said, alternating between watching the bubbles and the harbor entrance. There were three boats spaced evenly across the quarter-mile wide channel and several more were speeding in that direction.

"I have a horn mounted under the boat to recall divers" TJ said. "Don't know if it'll scare them or not."

"We have to try." Her voice broke as she tried to force herself to remain in control. "Look." She pointed to the boats blocking the harbor.

TJ moved his hand to the console and pushed a button several times. The muffled sound of the horn startled her and she looked around to see if the other boats had noticed. She looked down, scanning the water around the boat when bubbles erupted near the swim ladder and turned to tell TJ, but he had seen them. He pulled back the shifter to place the engine in neutral, jumped down to the deck and hopped over the transom. She sat there not knowing what to do while he stood on the swim platform and helped the men onto the boat.

"Goddamn, if you ain't trying to blow out my ears with that thing," Trufante said as he climbed onto the dive platform and spat the regulator from his mouth, revealing his trademark grin.

She smiled back, relieved the men were alive, and watched TJ pull

Mac out of the water and waited for Trufante to ditch his gear. It took both men to get Mac over the transom and onto the deck where he lay gasping for air.

"I can help him," she said and carefully climbed down the half-dozen steps to the deck. "Just get us out of here."

She went to Mac. His breathing was ragged, showing no signs of evening out. She felt the boat move and looked around for something to brace on. Suddenly Mac stopped breathing. She leaned over to check for an obstruction in his throat before starting mouth to mouth, but the bulk of the life preserver separated them. Adrenaline overcame her and she unbuckled the vest, placed it under his head and started to work on him, alternating between chest compressions and mouth-to-mouth. She began to tire and looked over the gunwale, but all she could see was the shore. They must be in the channel, she thought. She focused on Mac. Another breath and he coughed and spat seawater. She turned his head as he expelled another blast onto the deck. Relieved her training had actually worked she cradled his head.

***

Mac felt hands turning his head as he coughed up seawater. He tried to move, but another convulsion took him and he waited for it to pass. Finally the water was out of his lungs. He looked up at Alicia and breathed deeply. The situation came back to him and he sat up shaking the cobwebs from his head. She tried to stop him, but he fought her off and rose. The shore was close on both sides; he saw the tower of the castle on the right as they sped out of the channel. He thought they might be in the clear until they rounded a slight bend and he saw the blockade ahead.

He clenched his teeth, climbed the ladder to the bridge, and stood between Trufante and the other man surprised his legs held him. "What's the plan?"

"Ain't got one," Trufante said.

"There's a gap we can slip through if we can get there fast enough," the other man said.

Mac looked back at the deck to see where Alicia was. It was paramount to keep her safe, but the deck was empty. He assumed she was back in the cabin.

"Go for it," he said.

The boat picked up speed and the man corrected course, heading directly for the gap between the shore and the first boat. He looked back and saw several other boats coming towards them.

"We gotta get through that and into international waters."

"Yeah, TJ's the name, by the way." The man looked at him.

"You know the coast?" Mac asked.

"Hardly; I know the reef out of Key Largo. Don't think that'll help us here."

Mac studied the chart-plotter. There was little detail along the coast; comprehensive charts of the area were not yet available to US consumers. They would be out of the channel in less than a minute and he needed a plan. He looked up and studied the water just coming into view outside the harbor. An unbroken expanse of dark blue lay in front of them, showing no signs of the green and brown indicating a shallow reef.

"Straight out after we clear the boats," he called to TJ. He studied the blockade as they closed the gap, realizing the entire area was covered by the guns of a small naval boat. The barrels of the mounted weapons were already visible and he knew he had miscalculated. Just as he thought it, a shell hit the water in front of them.

"To port," he yelled at TJ. "We have to stay out of their range." TJ swung the boat towards the other side of the harbor mouth and Mac studied the other boats, looking for a weakness as another shell hit the water behind them. Several of the boats looked too small to hold any substantial weaponry, but they were close enough that they would have to deal with machine gun fire if they chose that course. There really was no option. He pointed TJ to a new route. The inaccuracy of the shells fired from the unstable platforms of the larger boat was less risky than what he was certain the machine gun fire would do to them. The hail of bullets was sure to damage the boat and probably hit a fuel tank, something they could not risk with miles of water between them and safety.

"The way they're turned, we'll be in his blind spot if we cross close to his port bow." Mac pointed at the ship that had fired on them. He could hear machine gun fire, but suspected they were out of range and focused on the course ahead. The boat was a hundred yards away. He could see the water churn as the captain tried to position his guns. Mac thought he was too late. They raced towards the gap, eyes focused on the blue water ahead. He heard the whistle of a projectile just before something exploded in the water.

THIRTY ONE

Seawater flooded the bridge, but quickly drained off. Mac turned to TJ. "No matter what - full speed!" he yelled. Bullets flew overhead and another missile caused a stream of water to splash off the transom. He jumped down to the deck to check for damage. Looking back before entering the cabin, he saw a line of boats converging on them.

"Alicia! Call for help." He entered the cabin and found two inches of water covering the deck. There was no escape; the boat was too slow, feeling sluggish as it plowed through the building seas. It would take a half-hour to reach international waters if they could maintain the twenty-five knots he estimated they were cruising, and that was if the Cubans honored the line. Right now they were at best a mile from the Cuban coast and the eleven miles to safety seemed liked crossing an ocean. There was no way they were going to make it unless he could change the playing field, but there was nowhere to hide in the open ocean, and he expected things to get worse. He entered the forward cabin and saw water pouring through a gash in the hull.

The hole, a jagged mess of fiberglass, was about a foot-and-a-half long and half as high, just at the waterline. Not disastrous if the seas were flat, but as they pounded into the waves, water flooded the boat. Mac guessed about fifty gallons a minute was pouring into the cabin, increasing with every wave that smashed the boat. Even now, at three thousand gallons an hour, the flow was twice what the standard bilge pump could handle. He braced himself as the bow hit another wave and heard a crack as more water poured into the cabin. The repair would be straightforward if they were not running from half the Cuban navy, but in their present circumstance they were in deadly trouble.

He left the cabin and sealed the door, guessing from the age of the boat that the cabin was constructed as a watertight compartment, but that was to isolate the damage and prevent sinking, not enable them to run at speed. Once the compartment filled, the bow would drop deeper and deeper into the water, unbalancing the boat.

For once he appreciated the life jacket wrapped around Alicia and called to her, "And watch that door. If water comes out, sound the alarm." She glanced up from the screen, a panicked look on her face, which grew worse as he stopped to grab two life vests from the netting above his head and took them with him.

"TJ," he yelled and exited the cabin. "Let Tru drive and help me. We're taking on water." The man instantly reacted and handed over the controls to the Cajun. In one step he was down the ladder and standing in front of Mac. "We took a hit from one of the missiles. Water is pouring in the forward cabin." Mac handed him a life vest which he let fall to the deck and threw the other to the bridge, where it lay ignored.

Mac didn't wait for the man to take action. "Do you have a spare bilge pump? Or pull the one you've got. That'll stem the tide, but we need to make a repair. Where are your tools?" Mac streamed off the questions and TJ reacted quickly. He went into the cabin and pulled the seats off the settee, dug through the compartment and handed Mac a small, battery-operated pump. It was rated for eleven-hundred gallons per minute, enough to help, but not solve the problem. "Get the wash down hose and we'll hook it up," Mac said, looking at the supplies in the compartment.

There were some tools and plugs for the through-hull fittings, but they were all too small to seal the gaping hole. He looked at the cushion TJ had tossed on the floor, grabbed it and opened the door. Water poured over the raised door sill. The hole looked slightly larger as Mac stuffed the cushion into it. The water slowed, but he knew the repair was only temporary. One wave could take it out.

"Here." TJ stood in the doorway staring at the damage to his boat.

Mac took the hose and attached it to the outflow on the pump. "We need some wire, about ten feet of two-strand." He unscrewed the lens from one of the cabin lights, the only source of power available, and pulled the fixture from the ceiling. TJ came back with two small spools of wire and a pair of cutters, handed them to Mac, and stood watching while he rigged the pump.

"I got this," Mac said. "Can you get an update from Tru and Alicia?"

TJ left him alone in the cabin. Bracing himself against the V berth, he waited out another wave before the boat settled enough for him to attach the wire. He turned the light switch on and the other fixtures dimmed, but the pump started to work. But the relief was short-lived. The waves had shifted the cushion and more water poured in. He stood there with the outlet hose in his hand and finally stuffed it in the hole. It was a start, but didn't solve the problem. He looked around for anything that could seal the hole. The surest way was from the outside, where the water pressure would hold the patch in place, but that was not an option. He heard an explosion close enough to shake the hull. The hole had to be patched from the inside. The seat cover was leaking badly and every wave enlarged the opening.

Surrender was always an option, but not one he cared to explore. He needed to get back to Marathon and help Mel. Another explosion rocked the boat. He went out to the deck. There were only two boats after them now, the smaller Zodiacs having turned back. The boats were too far back for him to see much detail over the white-capped waves, but from the age of the Cuban Naval ships he had seen, he doubted they could overtake them. They seemed to be matching speed, but at least for now, their missiles were falling short.

"What's our speed?" he yelled up to Trufante.

"Twenty-two; it's the best I can get from her."

Mac knew they could get another five to ten knots if he could stabilize the hull. That might make the difference between escape, and either death or a Cuban jail. He looked back at the boats chasing them and noticed the rows of dive tanks strapped to each side of the boat. There was something there, but it eluded him. Another shell exploded behind them, sending a stream of water onto the deck, this one a little closer than the last. The boats were closing.

He went back into the cabin and saw Alicia huddled in the corner, clutching her life jacket. Looking at her, he was reminded about all the ships that had sunk and the powerless passengers that awaited death or rescue. Then he knew what to do. The shipbuilders had started using ballast tanks and airtight compartments to keep ships afloat if they were damaged. Even the Titanic had floated for five hours before sinking. The tanks held the answer.

"I need some help," he called to Alicia, knowing she would be better off having something to do. "Find a knife and cut the cover off the cushion." She stared at him, her eyes wide with fear, but finally moved. He left her and went on deck. A quick glance confirmed the boats were closing. He heard the whistle of bullets flying around the deck. "One of you guys give me a hand," he yelled to the bridge. TJ jumped down the ladder, but just as he hit the deck, blood spurted from his thigh. He fell, clutching the wound and screaming.

Alicia emerged from the cabin and stood motionless staring in horror at the wound.

"Give me a hand here," Mac called to her trying to break the spell. He noticed a colorful beach towel left by a diver under the bench, grabbed it and wrapped it around TJ's leg. Blood quickly saturated it and he looked around for something to stem the tide. The towel was soaked and he feared the bullet had hit an artery. A dock line tied to a stern cleat was the closest thing at hand. He reached for it, inserted the line through the loop tied on the other end and placed it over the towel. With the line threaded backwards over the loop, he pulled tight enough to stop the flow, ignoring TJ's screams. Satisfied, he wrapped it around again and tied off the end. "Stay with him. You've got to keep him conscious," he told Alicia. He spotted the dive gear on the deck where he and Trufante had dropped it.

Bullets flew past, but he ignored them, and dragged the dive tank and gear through the cabin and into the forward berth. The boat shuddered again and he felt the concussion of a missile on the port side. With one motion, he hefted the weight of the tank and gear onto the berth. He unbuckled the BC, pulled it off of the tank and set it below the hole, trying to get everything prepared before pulling the cushion. Once he was ready, he removed the cushion ignoring the water gushing into the cabin. The bilge pump strained, but was worthless with the amount of seawater entering the boat and he tossed the hose to the side. He worked to maneuver the BC into the hole, but the weights still in its pockets caught on the opening, forcing him to waste valuable seconds while he pulled the vest back out and pulled the lead out. Water was streaming over the threshold.

"Alicia!" he yelled. Her face appeared in the open cabin door. "Tell them to raise the bow with the trim tabs."

"Trim what?" she asked.

"Trim the boat. Hurry, tell them." He didn't wait for an answer. Without the weights, he was able to place the BC in the opening and pushed the button to inflate the vest. Air rushed in and the vest expanded, filling the hole and stemming the flow of water. The boat responded almost immediately. Whether it was the trim tabs, the repair, or both, he felt it climb the waves, rather than crash into them. With the discharge hose for the bilge pump in hand, he left the cabin, wrapped the hose around the closest dive tank and watched the water pour into the ocean.

He ducked as a blast of water caught him off-guard, but noticed it had hit behind the boat. They had picked up enough speed to separate from the Cuban boats and he stood by the transom, catching his breath and watching the water behind them as several more shells exploded, each further away. From the bridge he heard Trufante yell in victory, but he knew they had a long way to go and a lot could happen before they got there. He turned his attention back to Alicia, who had TJ propped up against a cooler, helping him sip from a bottle of water.

"You going to make it?" he asked.

"Looks like we all will," he said. "Damn! A beer would be good after that shit."

Mac slapped him on the back, smiled at Alicia, and went to check the forward cabin. The floor was wet but there was no standing water, the pump able to pull the water out. The BC had only drips of water coming from it. He watched the repair when they hit another wave and realized the pressure against the damaged hull had stabilized the area.

"What's our speed?" he asked Trufante as he climbed the ladder to the flybridge.

"Damn near thirty knots – looks like we lost the buggers."

Mac looked behind and watched the boats fading in the distance, then turned to the chart plotter and noticed that the red dot marking their position was in international waters. The Gulf Stream had pulled them further east than he would have liked, making landfall in Key West difficult, so he set the cursor on Marathon and pushed the Go To button.

THIRTY TWO

The coast became familiar as they crossed the reef at Loo Key and followed Hawks Channel heading towards Marathon. Mac leaned against the railing, anxious now that they were getting close to Mel. The patch had held and TJ seemed to be OK. He would need a hospital, but the bleeding was under control and he was obviously not in shock from the way he was flirting with Alicia. They were almost home and he wondered if Mel was still alive, and if the entire ordeal had gotten him anywhere. Norm was dead and he was no closer to clearing his name than when they left. His only chance was the woman wearing the bright orange life jacket. Not a reassuring picture for his future.

"Can you two break it up for a minute," he said over the Jimmy Buffet music Trufante had blaring on the sound system. They looked at him as if he was ruining their party. "Alicia, I need your help."

She rose from the deck and Mac noticed their hands pause before they let go.

They moved into the cabin. "Norm made some promises. I did what he asked and need to see Mel," Mac said. They replaced the cushions on the settee and sat down.

"Oh." She paused. "With all this going on, I forgot to tell you."

"Tell me what?"

"I hacked into the hospital's computer." She paused again. "Yesterday, I think, and found some falsified test results from a bullshit doctor in Miami."

Mac stared at her, surprised by her language, waiting for her to

179

continue.

"I emailed a co-worker and asked him to check it out," she said and pulled the computer closer. The VHF was on the floor with an assortment of other gear that hadn't been secured.

Mac waited while she checked TJ's phone and set it next to the computer. "Don't you need the radio?"

"No, I've got four bars on the phone. It'll work as a hot-spot. Be faster too."

He waited while she worked through several screens and finally stopped to read. "Here. This is the response: Doctor handled and test results removed."

"That's it?" He was getting frustrated by the lack of information. "It's Saturday, isn't it?" he asked.

"I know. They are supposed to make a decision today," she said. "I can pull up her records."

"OK," Mac said and raced from the cabin, passing TJ on the deck and climbing the ladder two rungs at a time. "Head for Boot Harbor and turn in the canal by the hospital. Trufante nodded. "And shut that crap off. We're trying to run incognito here, you know. There might be a few folks looking for the boat that outran the Cuban Navy."

He went back down to the cabin, checking on TJ as he went. He nodded back and Mac glanced over the rail. The beach at Bahia Honda was off to the left, putting them about ten miles from the hospital. Alicia was working the screen when he returned and he was surprised to find the life jacket to the side.

She looked up as he sat next to her. "The test results have been removed and there is a note that her condition is unchanged. Treatment is pending a review by the ethics committee at four pm."

"What time is it?" he asked.

"Three," she answered. "Can we make it?"

"I think so, but I can't walk right in there like I came back from the dead." He slumped back in defeat.

"Actually, you can. You had the power to do that all along."

Mac stared at her. "What about what Norm said?"

"I'm sorry, but he lied about that, as well as everything else, to facilitate his plan. The worst that could have happened was you would be arrested, but even incarcerated, you would retain your role as decision-maker."

"So, let me get this straight. I can walk in the hospital, go to the meeting, and they have to listen to me."

"Exactly," she said and started typing. "I'll send the hospital an email and let them know to wait for you."

He set his hand over hers to stop her. "No. They'll have the sheriff there. Let me surprise them. After the meeting I can deal with whatever fallout I have to." He looked at her. "Don't suppose you can help me with that?" he asked.

***

Mac paced the deck as the boat passed under the old Boot Key Bridge and entered the mooring field. He looked at the canal leading to his house, but turned away and searched for the Thirtieth street canal off to the left. Trufante appeared to be steering right for it and he went to TJ.

"Can you put any weight on it?" he asked. "Hospital's right up there, but there's no dock and we're going to have to walk a few blocks."

TJ looked up at him and extended a hand. Mac hauled the man to his feet.

"I can put some weight on it. Hurts like all hell though," he said.

Mac looked around the deck and saw a boat hook latched to the gunwale. He released it from the bungee cords securing it and handed it to TJ. "See how that works."

TJ took a few tentative steps, using the hook for a cane, and sat on the bench. "It'll work."

They looked over the rail. Land was on their left and a grid of mooring balls, boats scattered on a few, were on their right. Trufante called out, turned the boat into the canal and eased the boat up to a dock.

"Stay with the boat," Mac called to Trufante and helped TJ get over the gunwale and onto the dock. "Hold on." He went to the cabin. "You should come with me," he said to Alicia. "I might need your skill-set."

She smiled and rose.

Mac helped her onto the dock and offered his shoulder to TJ. Together they crossed through several back yards and emerged on US 1. Mac could feel TJ's weight increase. They turned right and walked the two blocks to the hospital.

"Take care of him," he told Alicia as they entered the Emergency Room and he eased TJ into a vacant wheelchair by the door.

"Wait. They're required to report the gunshot wound," she said.

Mac thought for a minute. "Just tell them it was an accident. We'll deal with it later." He walked back outside and went to the main entrance, where he paused and looked down at himself before entering. His clothes were salt- crusted and torn. His body resembled a pincushion, lacerations across his arms and legs. He stood there shoeless, wondering who would listen to him, and then remembered he was coming back from the dead - might as well look like it.

With a deep breath, he entered the lobby and went for the restroom, where he did a quick clean-up job, then walked straight to the nurses' desk.

"Can I help you?" a nurse with a slight southern accent asked.

He couldn't help but notice the eyes on him. "Ethics committee meeting for Melanie Woodson?" he asked.

Three nurses gathered around and one, who carried herself with more authority, spoke. "And you are?"

He paused. "Mac Travis."

The words hung in the air for several seconds as the nurses looked back and forth between each other and him. "But the news reports…"

"Were slightly exaggerated." He couldn't help but borrow the Mark Twain quote. "Can you tell me where the meeting is?"

"Just a minute," the head nurse said and walked away.

There was an awkward moment before she came back, and the nurses and Mac exchanged glances. "They are in the meeting room on the fourth floor. I let them know you were coming," she said.

Mac left the desk, wondering who else she would tell he was alive. He didn't expect it to be this easy, especially with Bradley Davies involved. The elevator dropped him on the fourth floor and he glanced down the hallway to Mel's room, wanting to see her, but instead turned to the nurses' station and asked directions to the meeting room.

He stood outside the door, took a few deep breaths and turned the handle. Five pairs of eyes stared at him as he walked in, closed the door, and focused immediately on Davies. "You can go back to the hole you crawled out of. I'll take it from here." The line he had been rehearsing in his head came out better than he expected.

"Well, Travis, you're alive," Davies said.

"This is Mac Travis?" one of the doctors asked Davies.

"In the flesh," Mac answered for him.

"Then he can assume his role in the process," the doctor said and indicated an empty chair.

"Not so fast." Davies shuffled some papers.

"Excuse me?" the doctor said. "Miss Woodson was clear in her will."

Davies smiled and Mac waited. "There is a question of mental health here," he started.

Mac stared at him in disbelief.

"Mr. Travis has been running from the law for over a week, leaving a path of destruction in his wake. Y'all have seen the news." Davies slid into a southern drawl, trying to lure them under his spell. They could have been sipping lemonade on his back porch. "Look at him. Is this a man you would trust to make decisions about your life?"

"But ... " Mac started.

Davies cut him off and he noticed several of the doctors checking the clock on the wall. "I think a full psychological profile is in order before I am willing to allow Mr. Travis his position. What do you folks call it?" He pretended to think. "51-50?"

Mac stood speechless while the doctors talked amongst themselves. Finally one spoke, looking at Davies and not Mac. He knew this wasn't going his way. "We agree that a psych profile should be done before we change anything."

"Thank you. That's the responsible thing to do," Davies said. "Now, can we excuse Mr. Travis and finish our discussion?"

The doctor cleared his throat. "We have also agreed to continue life support until the determination about Mr. Travis is made."

Before Davies offer his rebuttal, the door opened and the sheriff entered. "Mac Travis. You are under arrest." He signalled to two deputies standing behind him. As Mac rose to comply, he could see the smile on Davies's face. They were about to leave the room when Alicia burst through the door.

"What's going on here?" she asked, her voice cracking slightly.

"Taking Travis to the station for processing, then I think these old boys want to 51-50 him. And you are?"

Alicia stumbled. "Alicia Phon, CIA," she said.

"You got credentials? It's my jurisdiction."

"No, sir," she said. "Mr. Travis is involved in an ongoing assignment with us."

The sheriff was silent for a moment. "I'll have to check this out." He turned to the deputies. "Take her too."

Mac saw Davies smile as a zip tie was placed on his wrists. Just before the officer had a chance to pull it tight, Alicia jabbed him in the ribs forcing him to raise his arms while she made a show of resisting.

"Good call, Sheriff," Davies said. "She doesn't look like any CIA agent I've ever seen."

"We'll sort this out at the station," the sheriff said, pushed Mac towards the door and walked him to the elevator.

The down arrow illuminated and there was a beep as the cab arrived. The doors started to open. Alicia suddenly threw her elbows up and pulled her hands free of the restraints. Before the deputies could react, she kicked the closest one in the shin, sliding her foot down the tender tissue. He fell in pain and she immobilized the other man with a chop to the neck. Mac mimicked her move, freed himself, then threw a roundhouse punch at the sheriff.

The doors opened and they entered the elevator, the lawmen too stunned to move. She pushed the door close button repeatedly and then the button for the second floor.

"Nice work," Mac said. "Is that what you hit me in the ribs for?"

"Can't believe the training actually worked," she said.

The doors opened on the second floor and they exited the elevator. Alicia took a glance at the exit plan posted above the call buttons and started running down the hall. "Come on. We'll take the back stairs."

"What about TJ?" Mac asked as he caught up to her.

"They admitted him. That's all we can do for now."

They reached the stairwell and were soon outside the building. Mac followed her back through the parking lot and into the neighboring yards they had crossed on the way there.

"Fire it up," He yelled to Trufante, who appeared to be sleeping on the bridge. He grabbed the dock lines, tossed them on the deck and jumped aboard. Alicia was just behind him. He heard the engines start and shift into forward. Seconds later they were moving towards the harbor.

THIRTY THREE

"That just got us in more trouble, but I guess we had no choice," Mac said as they left the dock and headed towards Sisters Creek. Although they were probably looking for him and Alicia by now, the boat, as of yet, did not have a target on it.

"They know you're alive now. Once the sheriff checks my credentials, we should be OK," she said.

Mac wasn't quite sure if OK was the right word, and figured resisting arrest, as well as assaulting an officer, would be added to the growing list of charges he would eventually face.

"At least it bought us a little time," he said. Now that he was alive again, they had agreed to delay the decision, but was it the right thing to leave Mel in limbo? He had thought until now that all he had to do was show up and she would be saved. He sat next to Alicia in the cabin, reading the notes on the screen. After reading the file, even with the bogus doctor's report, he wasn't at all sure what decision he should make or how he could make it. The one thing he did know was that he had to deal with Davies.

"Can you pull up what you can on Bradley Davies. Last I heard he was supposed to be in jail." Something slammed on the roof of the cabin and he heard Trufante call from the deck. He left Alicia studying the screen, went out of the cabin and climbed the ladder to the flybridge, carefully stepping around the blood dried on the deck.

"What we gonna do?" the Cajun asked.

"Hole up in Sister Creek until we can figure this out," Mac said, and sat in the chair next to him.

"I could use something to eat. We ran out of beer and chips a while ago."

"You guys can sure provision a boat," Mac jibed. "You know that canal at the end of Flamingo Key where we caught all that mullet. Head up in there and we can cut over to the Anchor. One of those Hogfish sandwiches that Rufus makes would sit good about now and Rusty will cover for us if anyone gets curious." His stomach grumbled at the mention of food.

"What about Mel?"

"I gotta figure that one out. The girl is working on clearing us with the sheriff and figuring out why Davies is roaming around the island like a free man."

"Why not just break her out," Trufante said, "like we did old Wood."

Mac almost laughed, remembering the old man, then realized Trufante had no idea how severe Mel's condition was. He decided to let the comment go and zoomed the chart-plotter in on the maze of canals they were about to enter. The canal he planned to tie up in was remote and he knew they could anchor in the vacant dead-end.

Alicia came out of the cabin and climbed the ladder. "No life jacket?" Mac asked.

She shot him a cocky look and leaned against the rail.

He looked at her and was proud, in a strange sort of way, of how she had grown in the last few days. She might have a future if they could get out of this mess. "You know that you don't have to follow this through. The threat to the ferry is over."

"I'm kinda liking hanging out with you two. Look at all the stuff I'm learning. If it's alright with you, I'd like to see justice, and that brings me to Bradley Davies. What a piece of work. He somehow got released under the sheriff's recognizance."

"It didn't seem like that at the meeting, more like the other way around. The sheriff was clearly answering to him," Mac said and thought for a minute. "Son of a bitch bought his way out of jail." Things were falling into place. "Mel knows every skeleton in his closet. He'd want to see her dead, if he could, before skipping the country."

They were quiet as Trufante wound the boat through the canals that were configured like a road system in a subdivision with docks lining both sides instead of cars. At the end of a dead end, he saw a house with its hurricane shutters in place and had Trufante pull up to the dock. Off to the side of the house they could see the mangrove-lined trail leading to the Rusty Anchor.

They climbed onto the dock and set off down the trail where after a quarter mile it opened up to a large crushed coral turnaround with the bar backed up to a turning basin leading to the Atlantic.

"Mac?" Rusty called when he saw them enter.

"Hey, Rusty, got a beer for a dead man?" Mac asked as they sat at a small table by the bar. "Rufus around? We could use a few of those Hogfish sandwiches."

Rusty brought over three beers and set them in front of the group. "Good to see ya, Mac. I knew all that wasn't true." He set the beers down and walked away.

Trufante was halfway through his beer when he looked over at Alicia's untouched bottle. "Better I handle that for you," he said. He finished his bottle in one swallow and grabbed hers. "Yo, Rusty, how 'bout a Coke for the lady."

"Watch the beers," Mac warned him. We're not out of the woods yet." Mac sipped his and thought while they waited for the food, trying to imagine what he would do if he were Davies. His reappearance along with a CIA agent would force Davies to make a move. Men like him would save their own skin first - but how? There was only one road off the island and he would have to go through Miami to leave the country. Boats were more common than cars here, but most were limited in range to the Bahamas, or maybe Cuba. That was it, he thought.

"With all these new agreements with Cuba, did they agree to an extradition treaty?" he asked Alicia.

"I don't think so."

The food came and they dug into the famous sandwiches. Mac heard the buzz of a small plane flying overhead, about to descend into Marathon Airport, and he knew the answer. The airport had few commercial flights now, but was a hub for private planes. If Davies could rent one, he could be out of the country by dark.

Mac shoved the rest of the sandwich in his mouth and went to the bar, "We need a check and a favor."

"It's on me. Just glad you're still with us. How can I help?" Rusty asked.

"We need to get over to the airport quick?"

Rusty dug around under the counter and handed Mac a set of keys. "Julie's deployed. Just don't screw it up."

"I owe you big for this." .

"No worries, we got to take care of each other."

Trufante stood up and slugged the rest of the beer before he and Alicia grabbed what was left of their sandwiches and followed Mac into the hot sun. They saw the car across the lot in front of Rusty's house. Once in, Mac spun the wheel and turned towards the narrow driveway between the Keys RV Park and the end of Sombrero Beach road. They drove through the vacant lot and turned right on US 1, passed the road to Trufante's apartment. The runway came into view on the left. A small plane was taxiing and Mac accelerated, hoping they were not too late. He pounded the wheel waiting for several trucks to pass before he could turn left onto Aviation Boulevard, and then made a quick right on the frontage road. The needle was close to eighty miles an hour before he braked at the general aviation terminal.

"Wait," Alicia put a hand on his shoulder, "let me do this. I can get more information than you can. If you guys go in there looking like this, no one's going to talk to you."

Mac nodded and relaxed his hold on the door handle. "You're right." He sat back in the seat with the air-conditioner blowing on his face and waited for Alicia to return.

Less than a minute later, she ran from the building. He opened his window and was ready to get out when she ran past him, opened the back door and got in. "That's him!"

Mac followed her pointed finger to the small twin-engine plane pulling onto the runway. The Cessna was still on the taxiway, about to make its turn at the eastern end of the runway.

"Take the car and try to cut him off," he yelled at Trufante, who slid behind the wheel as he got out. A water truck was parked twenty feet away, its engine running the pump to fill its tank from the hydrant next to it. Mac raced to the truck, skidding to a stop just long enough to disconnect the hose, then ran to the driver's door and jumped in. He jammed the truck into gear, and dragging the hose behind him, headed to the far end of the runway.

He could hear the pilot increase the RPMs of the engines and watched the plane shimmy back and forth as he braked, building power for take-off. Mac cut the wheel, turning hard to make the sharp turn from the frontage road to the runway. Two-thirds down the tarmac, he stopped the truck, jumped out and ran for the hose. The plane was moving down the runway, picking up speed as it approached. Mac closed the valve at the end of the hose and went for the control panel on the truck. He turned the pump on full, hoping there was enough water in the tank to stop the plane. The hose bucked as it pressurized and he ran towards the end, dodging the line as it swung towards him. Filled with water, it stopped moving and he grabbed the nozzle and opened the valve. High pressure water blew from the nozzle. He clamped the hose between his legs and aimed towards the grass.

He waited, spraying the half-dead grass, not showing his intentions until it was too late for the pilot to turn. Finally, when the plane was fifty feet from him, he turned the full pressure of the water on it. The plane swerved and skidded sideways as the pilot lost visibility and fought to control the craft on the slick runway. One of the engines cut out, probably from the water, and the plane spun on the tarmac, coasting to a stop on the grass.

Mac closed the nozzle, set the hose down and ran for the passenger door. The pilot already had his door open and was half way out of the plane, but he was of no concern.

He reached the plane and climbed the strut. Before he could reach the door, Davies opened the hatch, slamming the thin metal into him in an effort to dislodge him from the plane, but the door was too light to do any damage. Mac took the opportunity to slide down the strut and lean over backwards, grabbing Davies in a grip between his legs. With anger built from a week of hell, he squeezed and pulled the man from the plane, flipped him, releasing the grip with his legs at the apex, watching as Davies body slammed into the hot tarmac.

He walked past the growing crowd of people surrounding the body, barely casting a glance at Davies and walked to the car.

THIRTY FOUR

Mac felt uneasy and a little scared that the Sheriff had posted a guard, but he walked through the door of the hospital ready to face whatever lay in his way. His resolve took him past the admittance counter and to the elevator. As he waited, he glanced over his shoulder, expecting to be confronted, but the up arrow lit and the doors opened. He moved to the side and then entered after a nurse wheeled out a man in a wheelchair. One more obstacle stood in his way and he breathed out. No one was waiting for him outside the elevator, in the hall or at Mel's door. He entered her room and paused. White coats were clustered around the bed. His hopes fell.

A nurse brushed past him with a tray and he was about to ask what was going on, but thought better of it. The group worked frantically around the body on the bed. Mac stood glued to the window, watching, until suddenly they stopped. His stomach dropped, feeling powerless to do anything. Two doctors left the group and exited the room. There was something about their demeanor that he didn't understand. He looked back in the room, his eyes drawn to the signal on the heart monitor. Instead of the flatline he expected, it bounced up and down.

"How is she?" he asked the doctor, who he recognized from the ethics committee.

"She's out of the coma and reacting to treatment," he said and turned to go, but paused. "Thanks to you. That DC lawyer and his phony doctor almost had us pull the plug."

"Can I see her?"

190

"Go on in. I don't think she is coherent enough to recognize you, but she's strong. It might take a little time, but I expect she will recover."

Mac thanked him, tentatively walked into the room and went towards the bed. The nurses were fussing over her IV bag and sensors, but they moved aside to let him approach. He went to the side of the bed, feeling out of place and not knowing what to do. Her hand lay beside her body and he picked it up and looked at her face. Her eyes were closed, but the breathing tube was gone. A spark went through him as he felt pressure on his hand. He looked down and her fingers were moving, trying to grasp his. He gently squeezed back and thought he saw a smile cross her face.

He stayed with her until a nurse tapped his shoulder, indicating it was time to leave. He squeezed her hand one more time before moving out of the way and left the room, feeling unnatural, like he was walking on a cloud, the adrenaline of the last week draining with every step.

He walked out of the hospital, wondering what was next when an ambulance pulled up and shut off the lights and siren. He re-entered reality when the back door popped open, the EMTs jumped down and slid the stretcher out, expertly opening the carriage and dropping the wheels. Two men ran out of the hospital and helped the medics wheel the stretcher in. Mac looked down at the body and saw Bradley Davies, eyes open, looking back at him. Mac didn't know whether to be happy or sad.

The ambulance driver closed the doors and pulled to the side, leaving a space for the sheriff's car that had just pulled in to park. Mac kept walking but heard the sheriff call for him to stop. At some point he had to face him.

"You got lucky this time, Travis. That young-un really is CIA."

Mac stood there facing him, waiting for him to finish.

"I got my eye on you: best watch your step."

***

Mac parked his new, beat up pickup, in front of the dive shop and went towards the source of the music. It had been an up-and-down few weeks bouncing back and forth between Miami, where it seemed like he had spent a lifetime. First a suspect, and later a witness testifying to Norm's escapades, then back to Marathon to be with Mel as she recovered. Alicia had been instrumental in getting him back on his feet, after first bailing herself out of trouble. His boat, where he now lived, had been returned and sat at his dock. He hated staring at the wreck of the house, but fortunately it was covered by insurance and would soon be rebuilt.

"Yo, Mac!" TJ called from the bridge. "Check out the front end."

Mac waved to him and Alicia, who emerged from behind TJ, and walked to the bow where he inspected the repair. A freshly painted jagged red line traced the repair, like a badge of honor. He gave TJ a thumbs up and walked back to the stern, tossed his gear bag over the gunwale and hopped on board, where he was met with a bear hug from Trufante.

"How's Mel?" the Cajun asked.

"Doing good. They expect to release her any time." Mac took the offered beer.

Mac, Alicia and TJ went up the ladder to the bridge while Trufante tossed the lines to the dock. The boat inched away from the pilings and turned towards the canal and open water.

"No life jacket?" Mac asked.

"I thought you said I was boat-worthy now." She laughed. "TJ's teaching me how to dive too."

They stood together on the bridge as the boat came up on plane and headed to the reef. Twenty minutes later, TJ pulled back on the throttles and yelled at Trufante to throw a buoy. He skillfully circled the marker, checking the depth finder to verify the contour of the bottom was right, and pulled forward into the current before calling to Trufante to throw the anchor. The boat settled back as he paid out line and stopped right by the buoy.

Mac had spent countless hours underwater, but most of it was work. He had done little recreational diving over the years and he experienced the thrill of the crystal clear water and colorful fish as if for the first time. He had no purpose other than to enjoy the dive. TJ was several feet away, running Alicia through the safety procedures required for certification. She had her mask entirely off and he watched her put it back in place, tilt her head back and clear the water. He could see the smile in her eyes when she finished the routine and TJ nodded and led them over the reef. They were diving one of TJ's secret spots right on the edge of Pennekamp State Park, an underwater reserve off Key Largo. Mac was amazed at the numbers and size of the fish, especially the snapper and grouper, who somehow knew they were protected here. He floated over the coral formations, admiring them as he followed TJ and Alicia. It had seemed short, but TJ signaled for them to surface. He checked his new watch and noticed it had been almost forty minutes.

Back on board, they sat back and let the sun dry the water from their bodies.

Trufante broke the silence. "Y'all got some kind of private club going on down there. Come on up and bring me a beer."

They gathered around the helm. "So I heard Davies is out of the hospital and back in jail," Mac said, relaying the information one of the nurses had shared with him. "Don't expect it'll be one of those country club places this time. But somehow that guy always lands on his feet. Don't think we've heard the last of him."

"Son of a bitch has more lives than me," Trufante said.

Mac checked his watch. "It's been an hour. Ready to get wet?"

I want to extend a special thanks to my fellow Florida Keys author Wayne Stinnett for the use of his characters and places. Wayne and I released our first books weeks apart and unknowingly made our main characters neighbors. It only made sense, since they lived in the same place around the same time that they would know each other. It has been a lot of fun working Jesse, Rusty and the Anchor into the book.

Check out Mac and Wood in Wayne's latest novel: <u>Fallen Honor</u>

47304960R00120